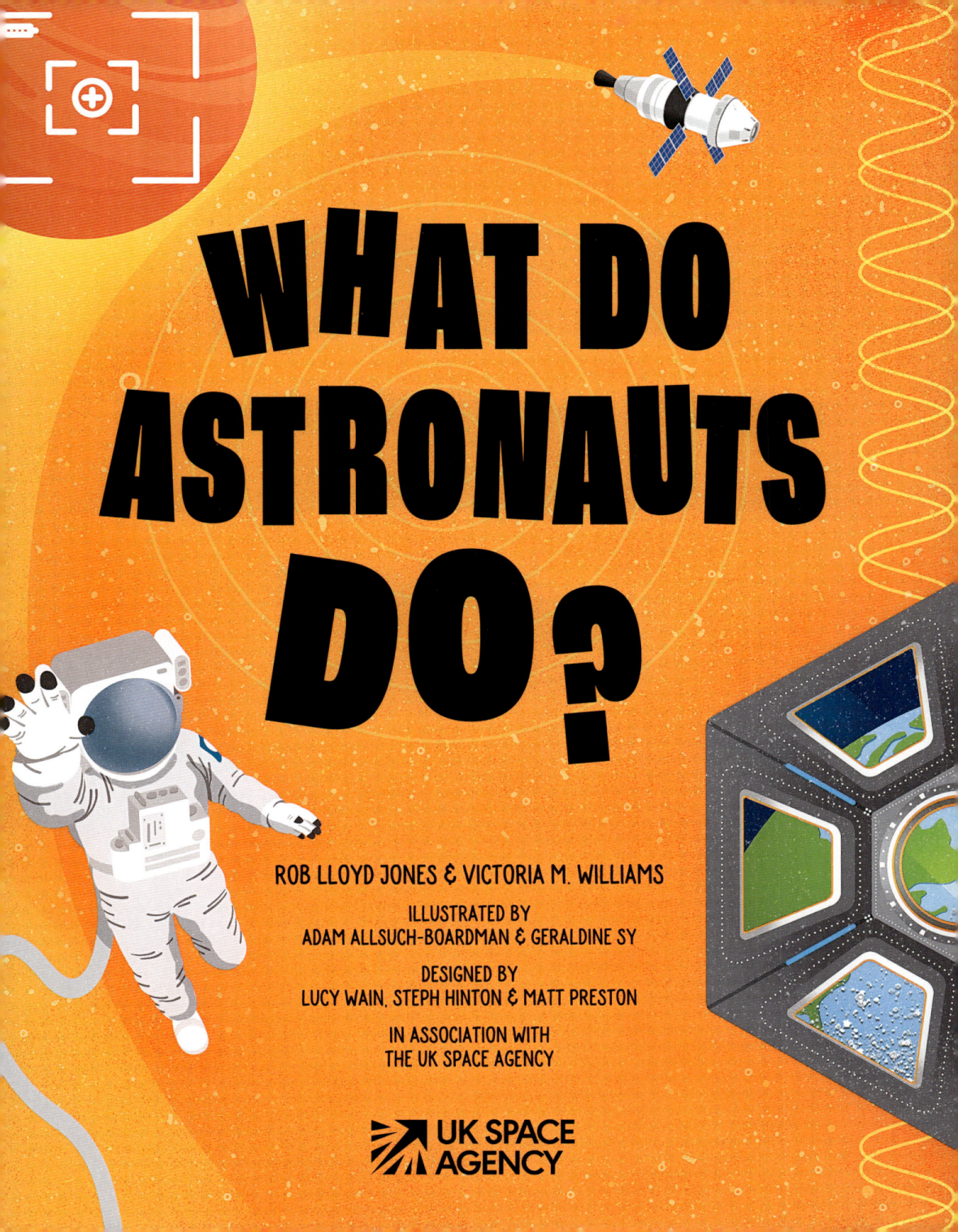

Contents

Introduction	4
Space mission training	8
Building spacecraft	22
Up, up and away!	30
Living in space	40
Space science	52
Exploring further	62
Becoming an astronaut	74

WHAT **DO** ASTRONAUTS DO?

Have you ever dreamed of blasting off into space to explore the universe? You can do just that, if you become an astronaut.

Are you fascinated by space but prefer to stay on Earth? Sending astronauts and equipment into space is a challenge that takes HUGE teams of people, all working together. So, there may be another space job to suit you.

In fact, there are so many jobs to do with space that the whole area is known as the SPACE INDUSTRY.

There are people working right now on all sorts of space-related topics...

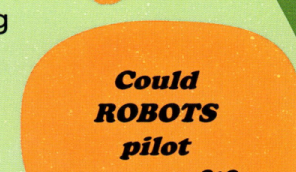

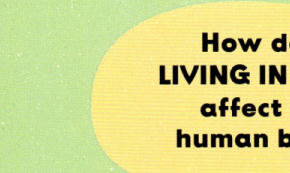

Who to work for...

If you become an astronaut, you'll be working for a space agency – a government organization in charge of space exploration. Which agency you'd work for depends on where you live...

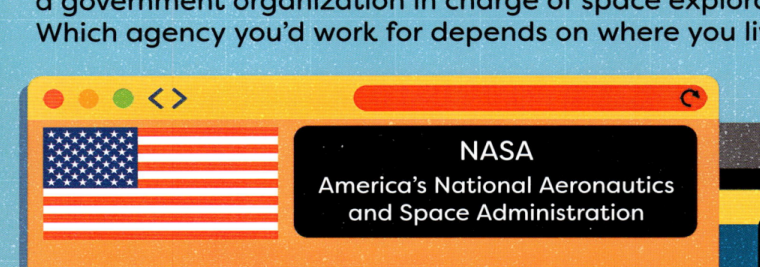

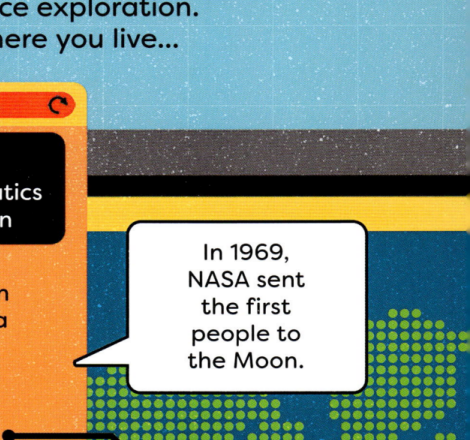

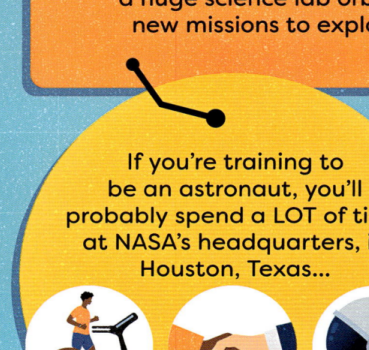

ROSCOSMOS

Roscosmos organizes space activities for Russia, where astronauts are known as **cosmonauts**. Roscosmos built part of the ISS, and trains astronauts at their training base near Moscow.

CNSA

China National Space Administration

In China, someone who travels into space is known as a **taikonaut**. CNSA built a space station called Tiangong (which means Sky Palace), which is in orbit around Earth.

If you want to work in the space industry WITHOUT becoming an astronaut, you have more choice.

The big government agencies run the biggest missions, but many universities and private companies do space research and develop new technology.

JAXA

Japan Aerospace Exploration Agency

JAXA sends satellites into orbit, designs new tech for space travel, and plans missions to explore asteroids and the Moon.

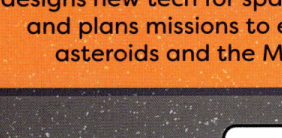

JAXA also helped to build the ISS.

Space agencies hold recruitment drives for new astronauts. To apply, you'll need to study hard and be physically fit.

And if you're lucky enough to be taken on as a trainee, it's just the beginning...

Basic training

Welcome to astronaut training. The first part is called **basic training**. It's not at all basic, but it is fascinating. You'll work with SPECIALIST INSTRUCTORS as you start to prepare for missions into space.

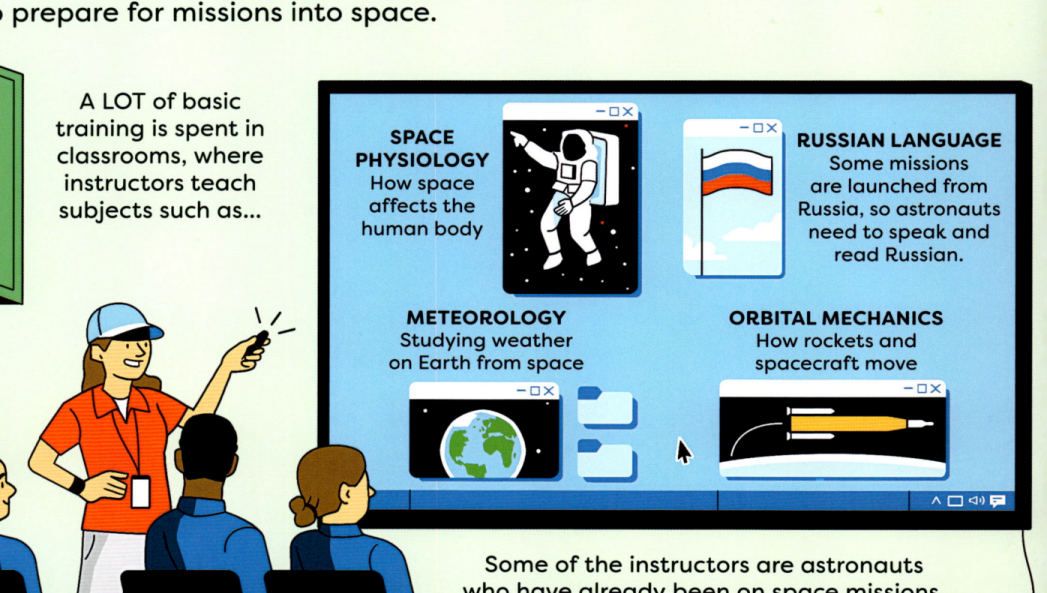

A LOT of basic training is spent in classrooms, where instructors teach subjects such as...

SPACE PHYSIOLOGY How space affects the human body

RUSSIAN LANGUAGE Some missions are launched from Russia, so astronauts need to speak and read Russian.

METEOROLOGY Studying weather on Earth from space

ORBITAL MECHANICS How rockets and spacecraft move

Some of the instructors are astronauts who have already been on space missions. Others are specialists in a particular area.

Next, you have to pass strict fitness tests to prove you're ready for the physical demands of space travel.

In one test, trainees have to swim three lengths of a 25m (82ft) swimming pool, wearing clothes and shoes...

...and then tread water for ten minutes.

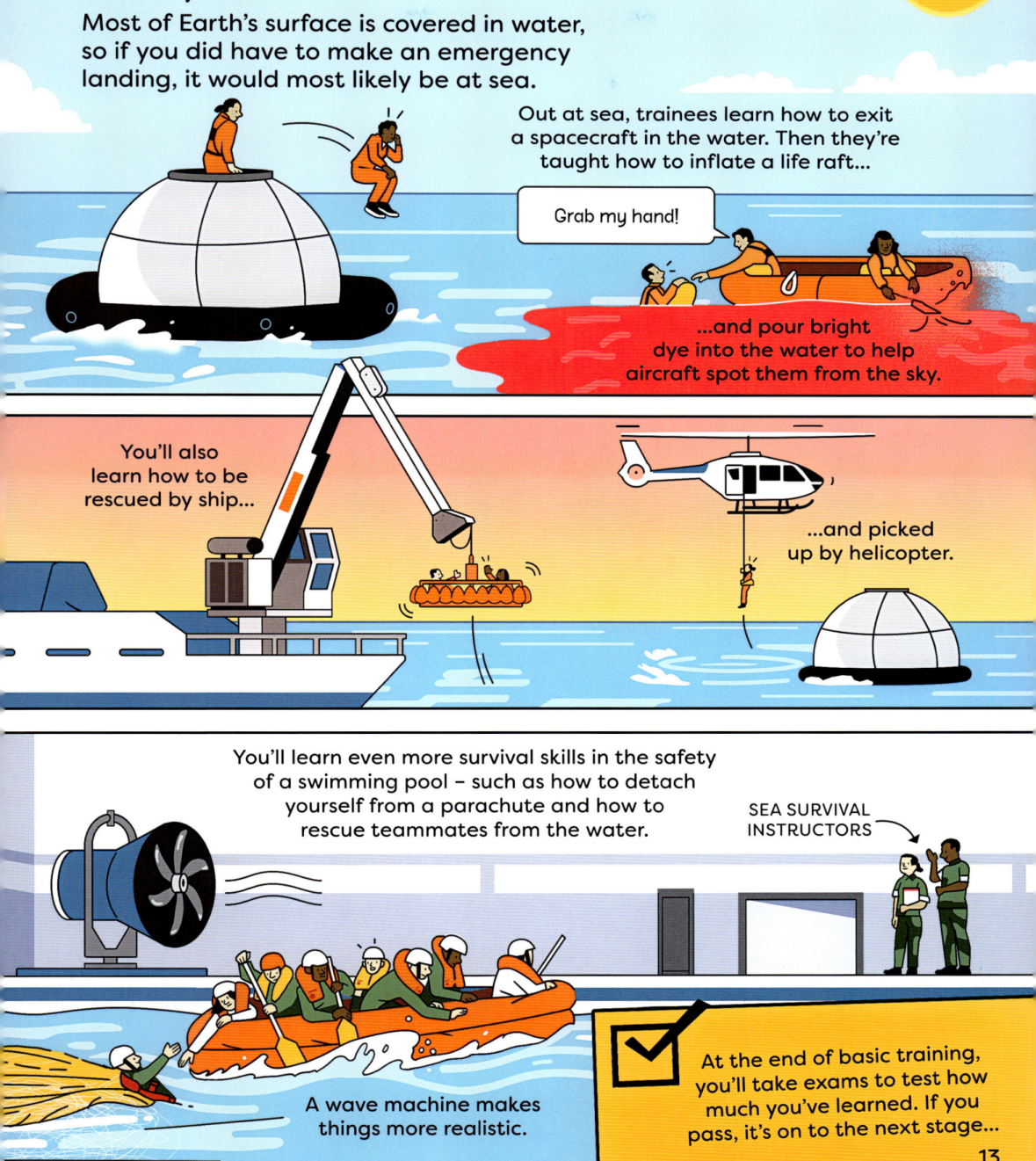

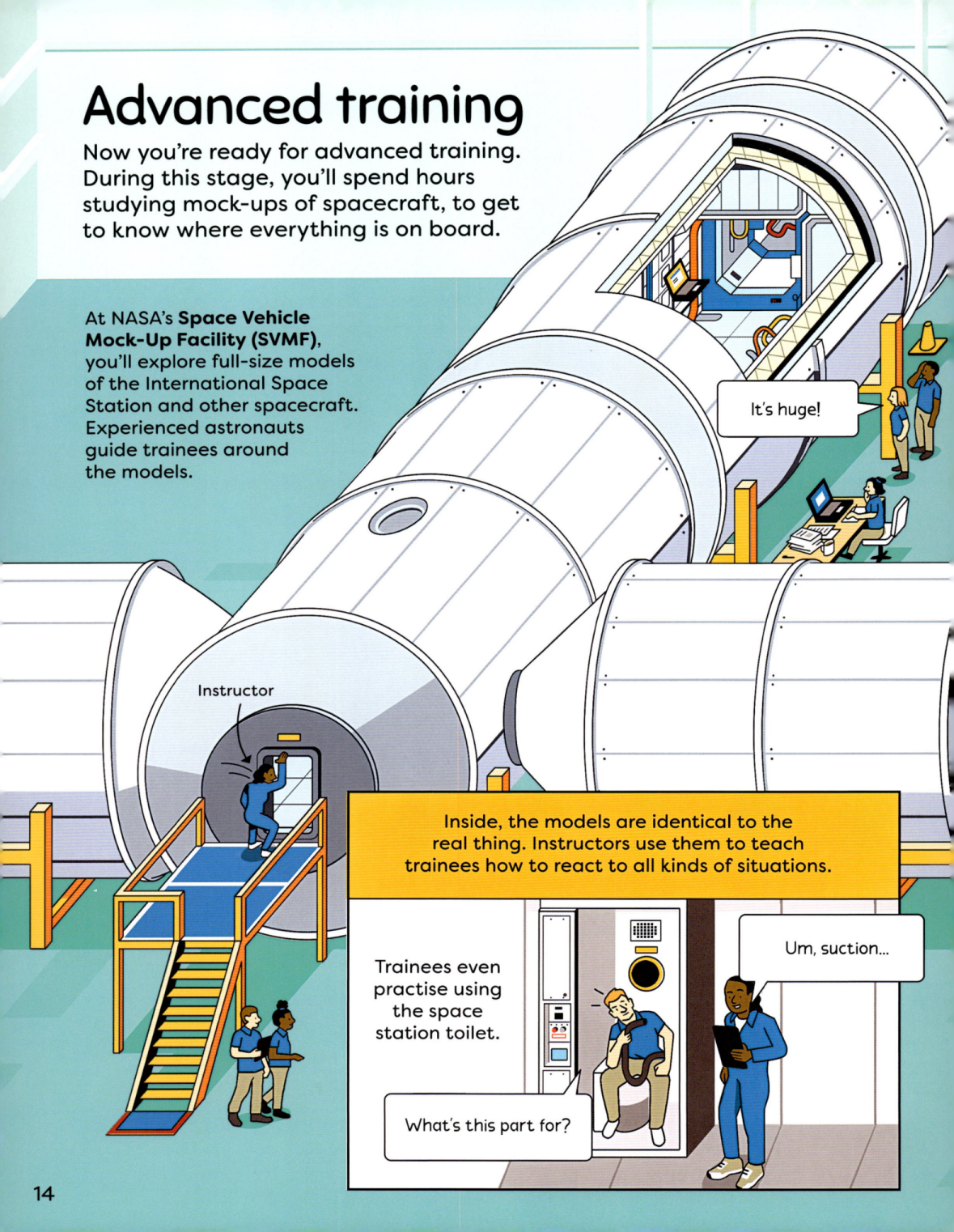

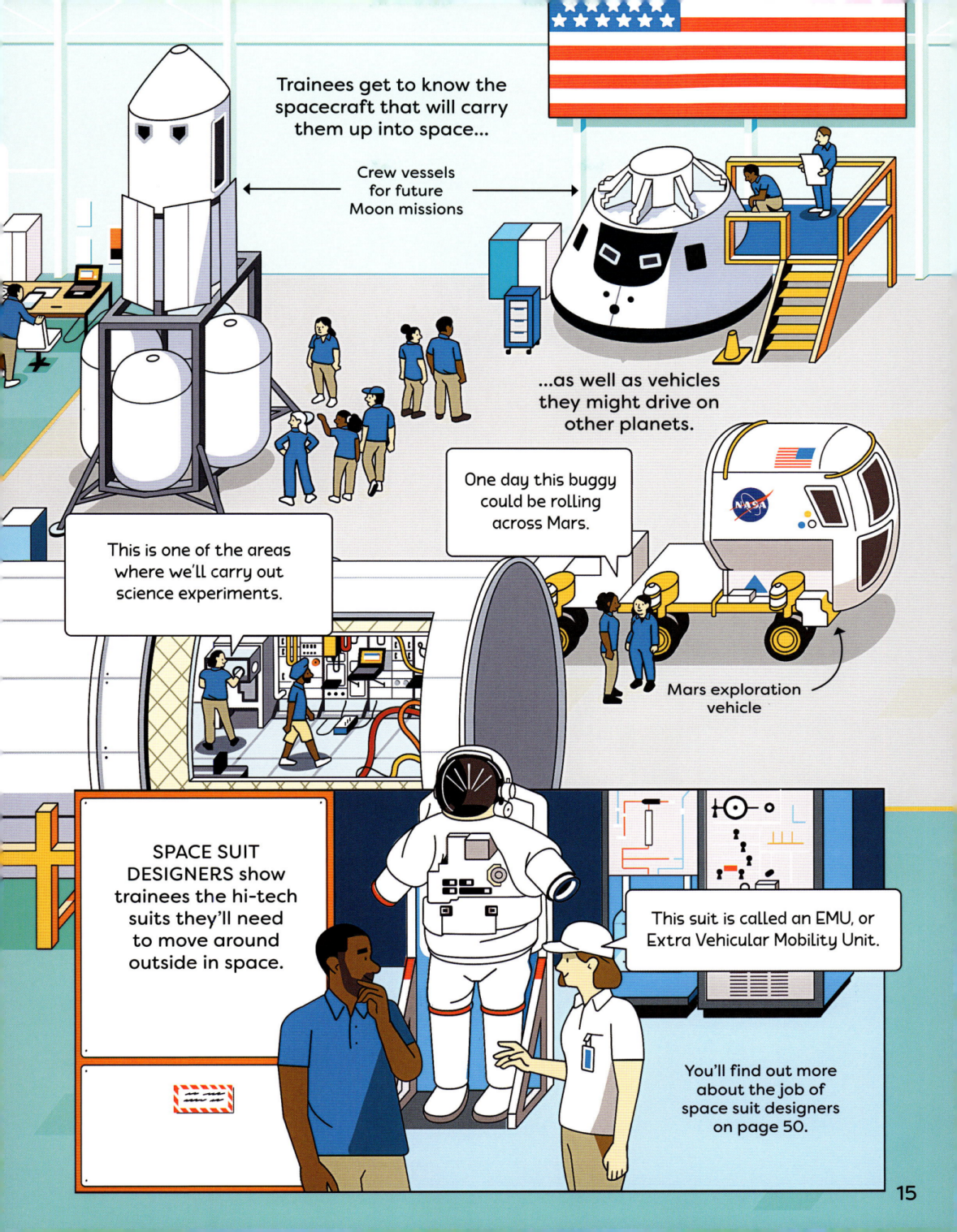

Microgravity

If you go into space, you'll experience something incredible – the feeling of weightlessness that makes everything seem to float. This is called **microgravity**, and you'll train for it while you're still on Earth.

What causes microgravity?

On Earth, gravity is the force that makes things fall to the ground. As you travel away from Earth, this effect slowly fades – but it seems to vanish much sooner if you go into orbit.

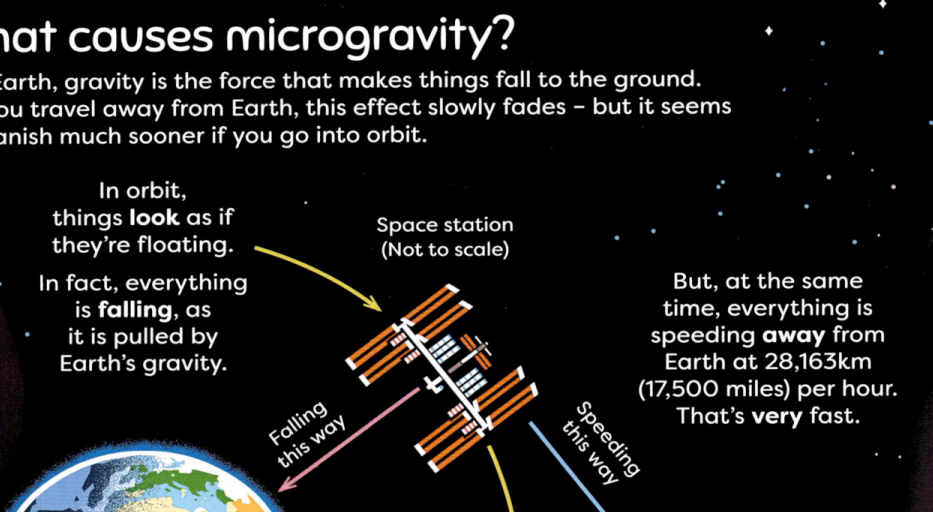

In orbit, things **look** as if they're floating.

In fact, everything is **falling**, as it is pulled by Earth's gravity.

But, at the same time, everything is speeding **away** from Earth at 28,163km (17,500 miles) per hour. That's **very** fast.

Trapped between the two forces, things fall **around** the Earth, not down to it. This is called being in orbit.

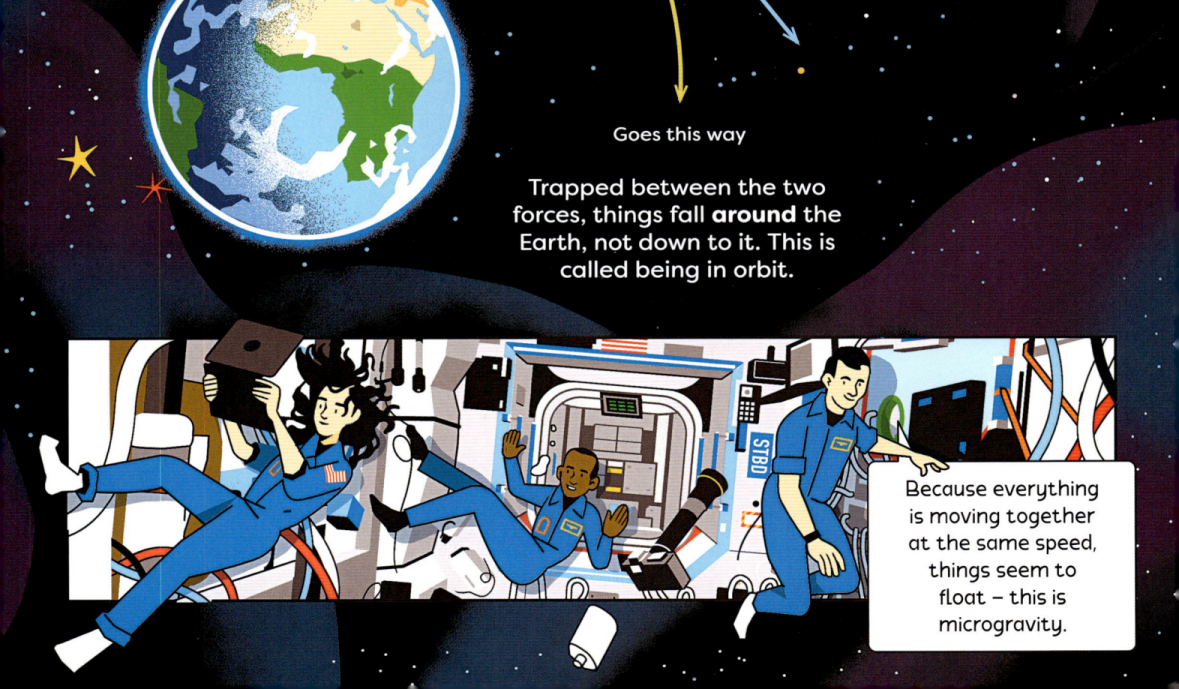

Because everything is moving together at the same speed, things seem to float – this is microgravity.

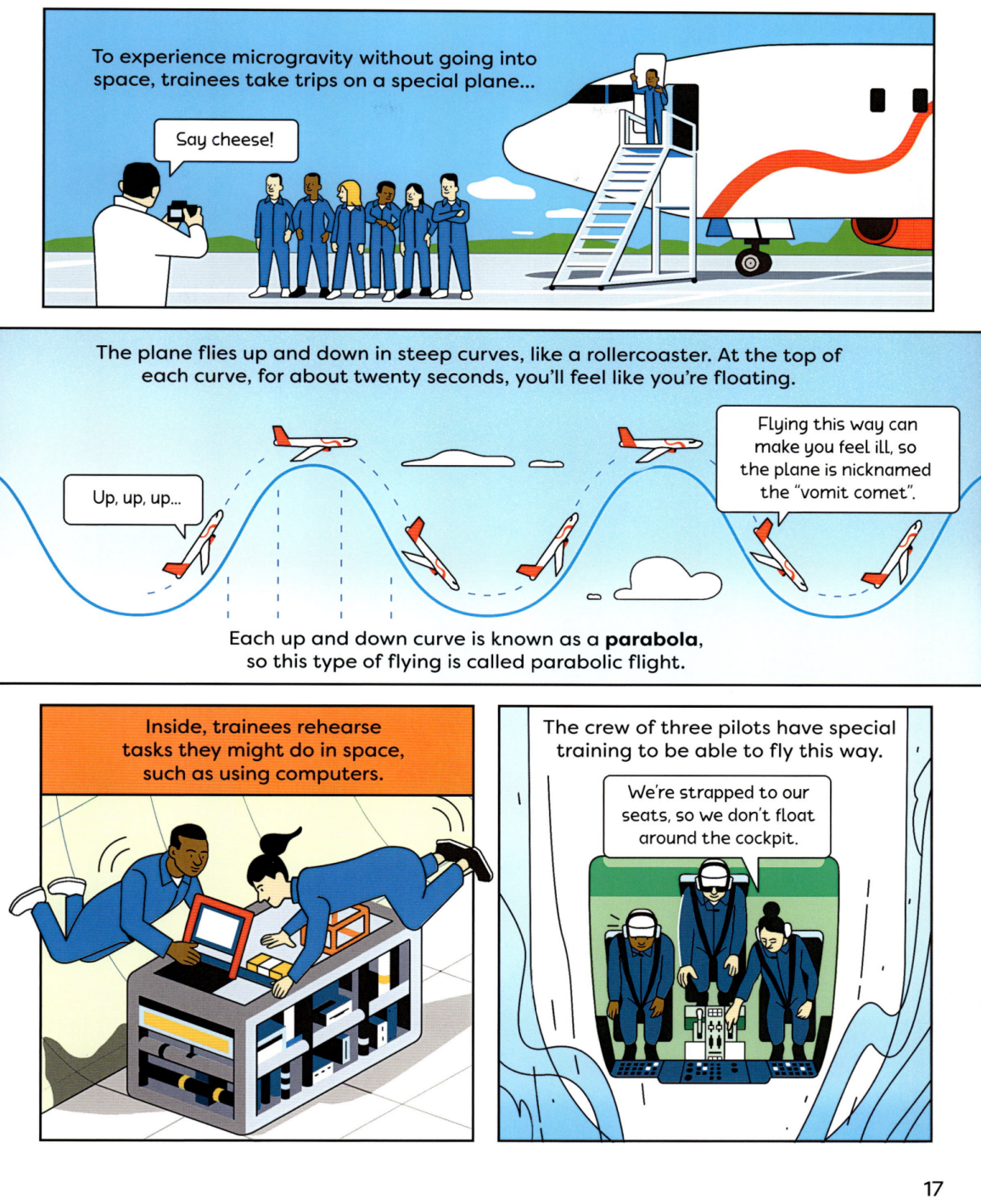

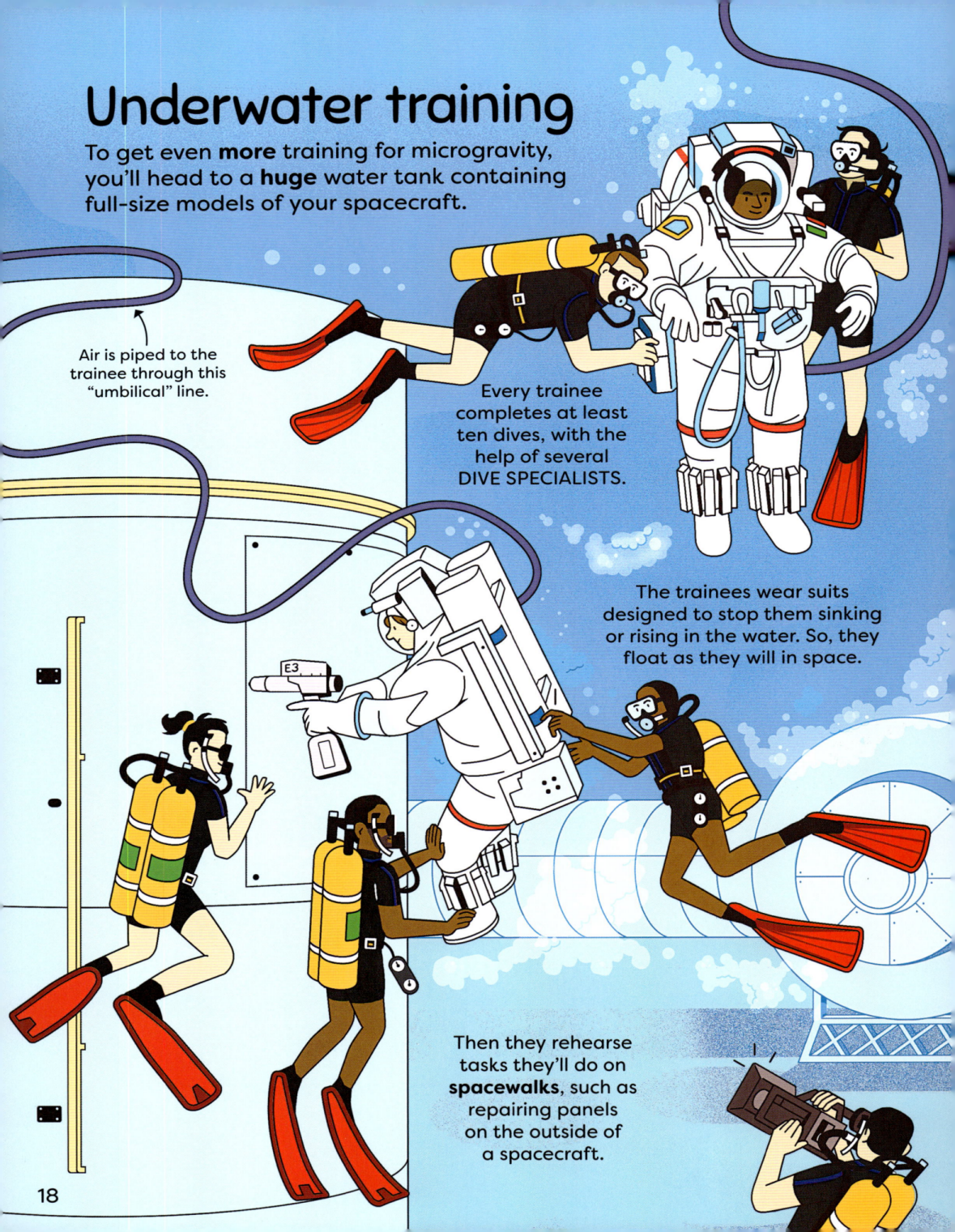

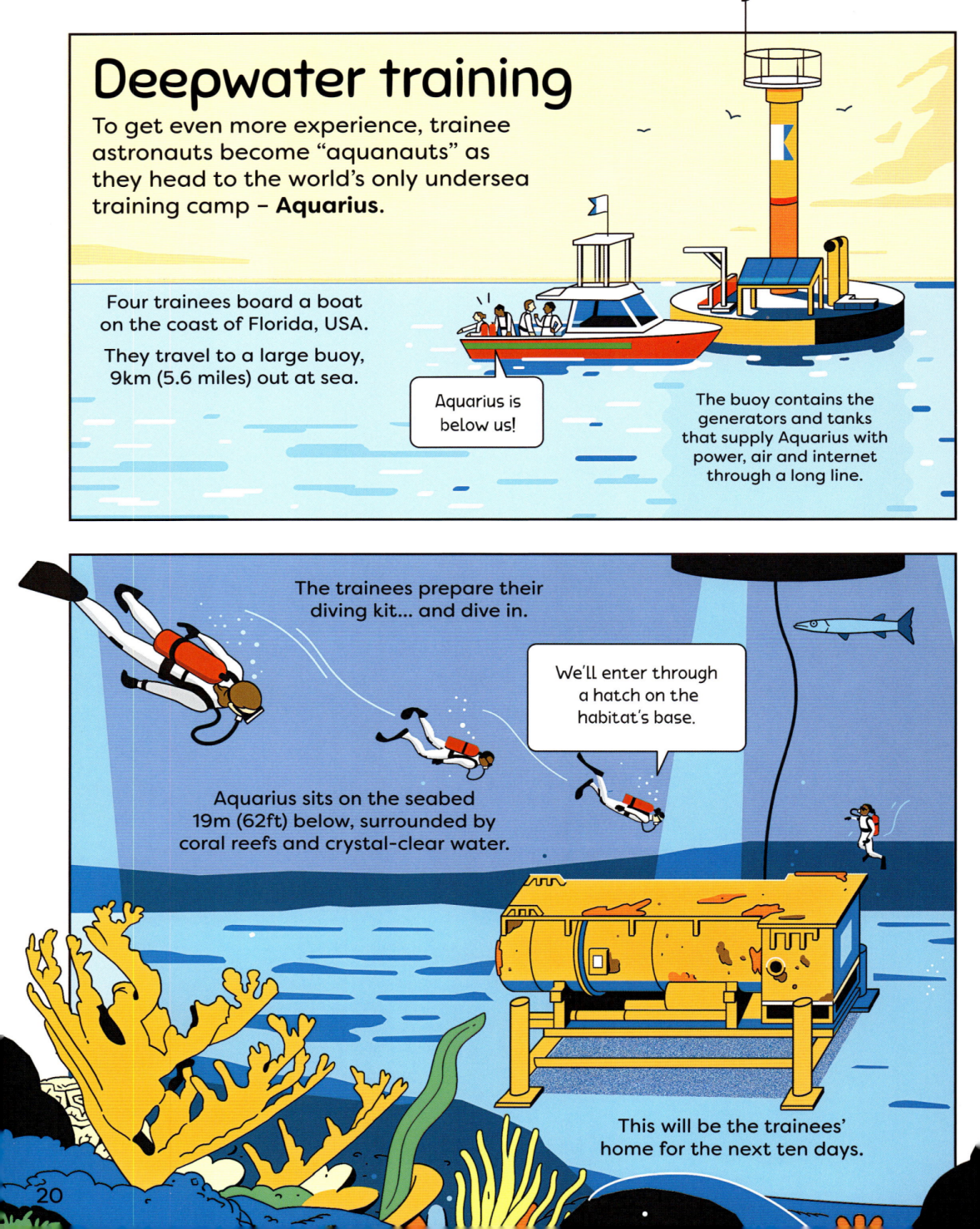

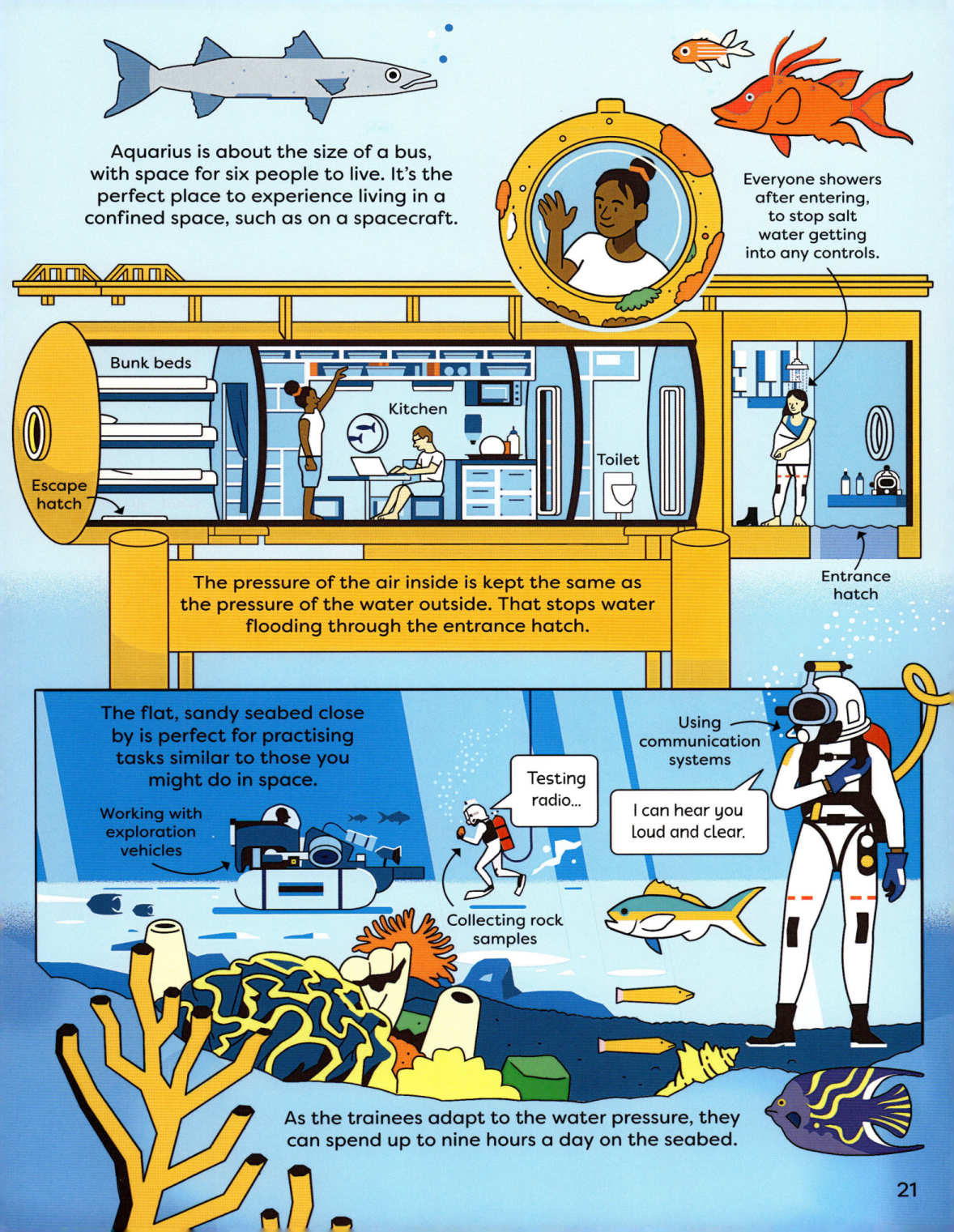

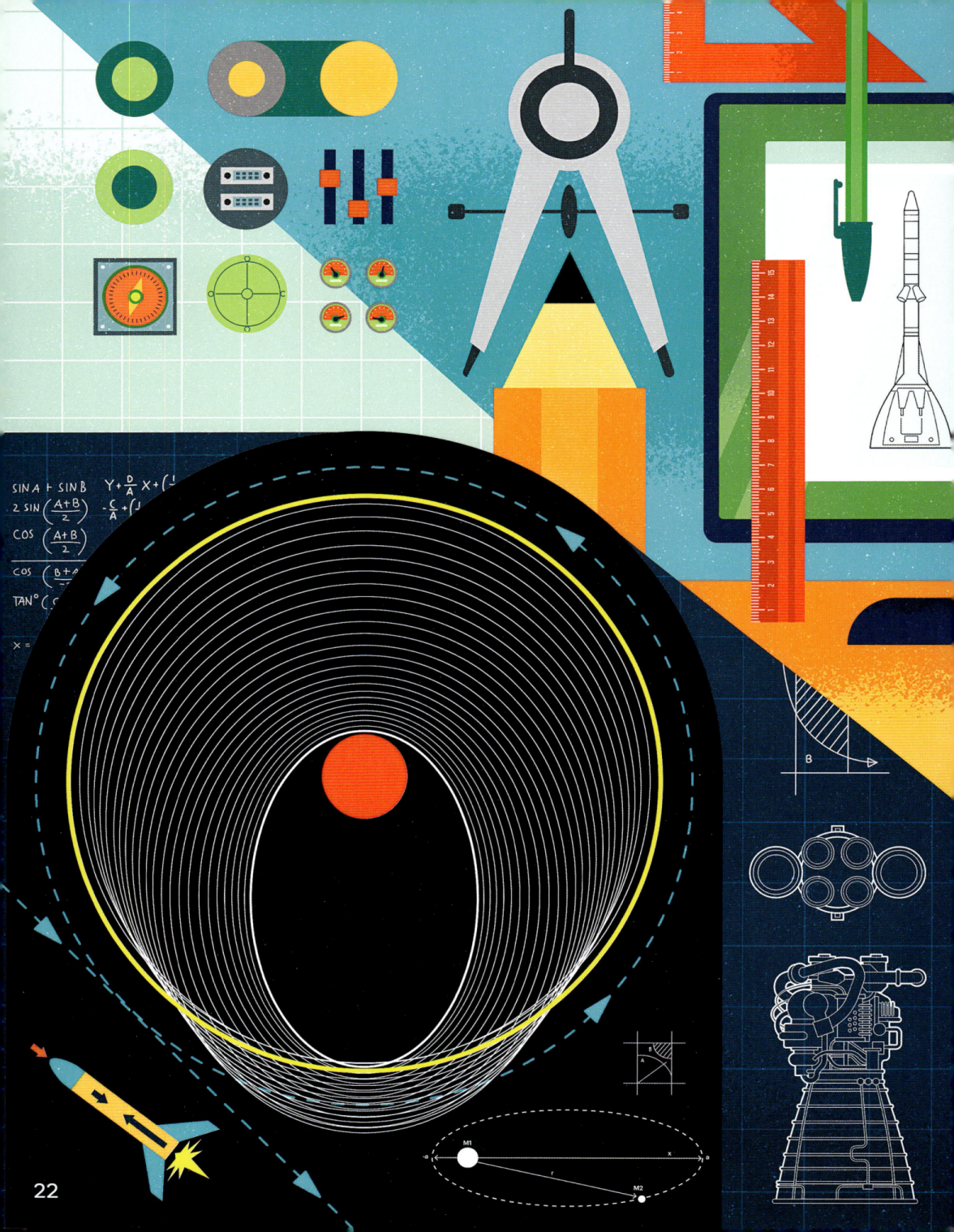

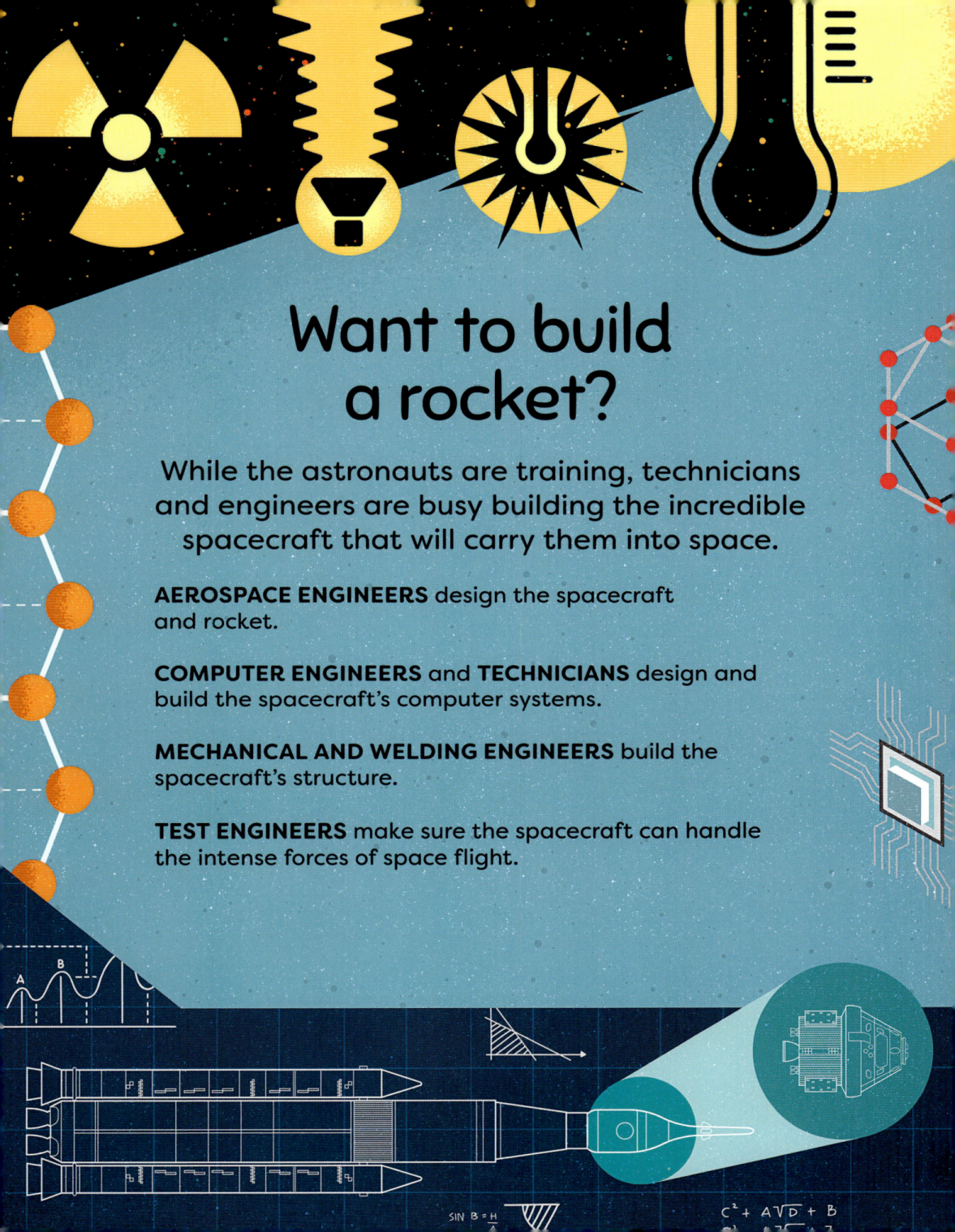

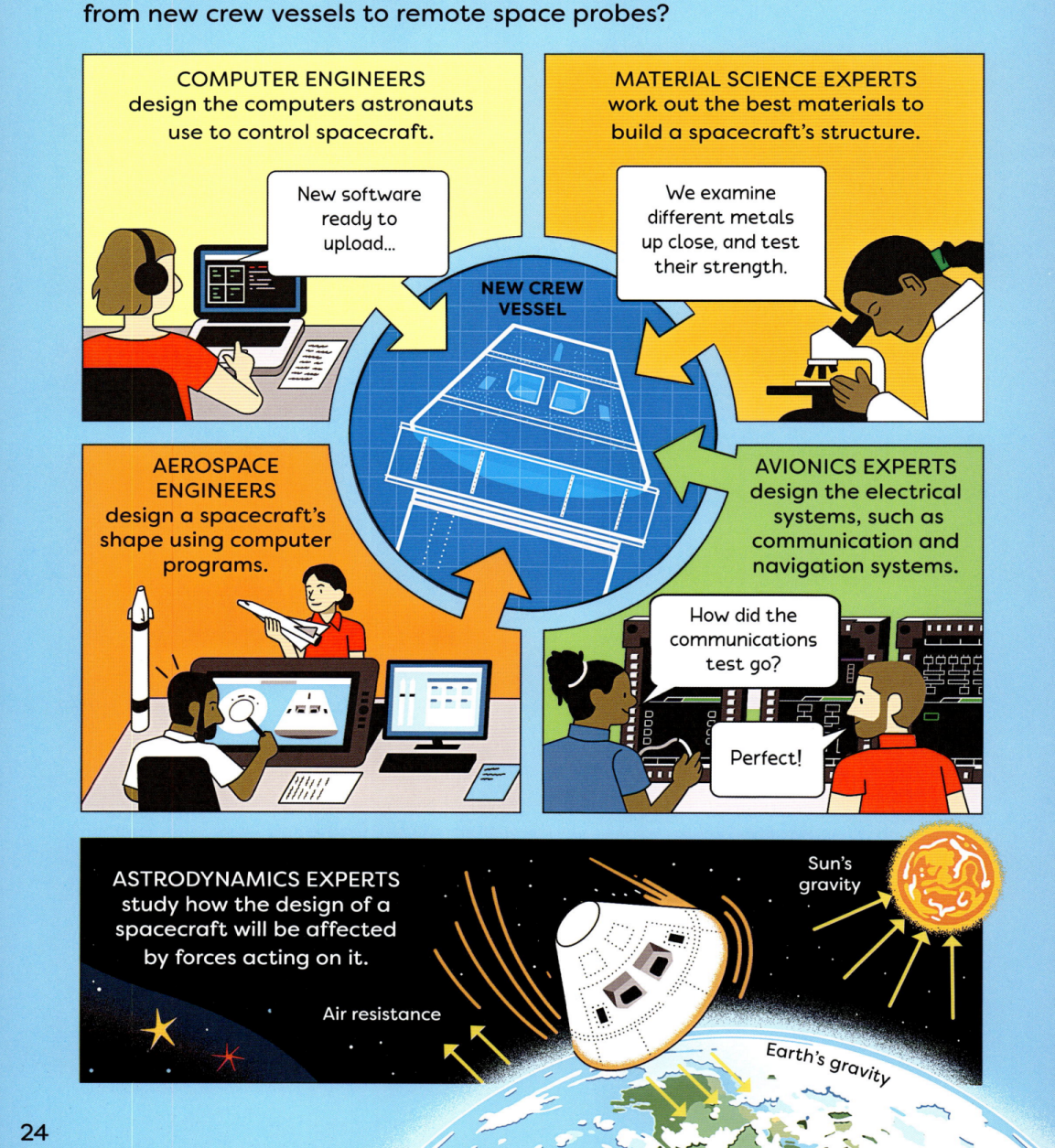

Building the structure

Now the spacecraft is designed, it's time for MECHANICAL ENGINEERS to get to work.

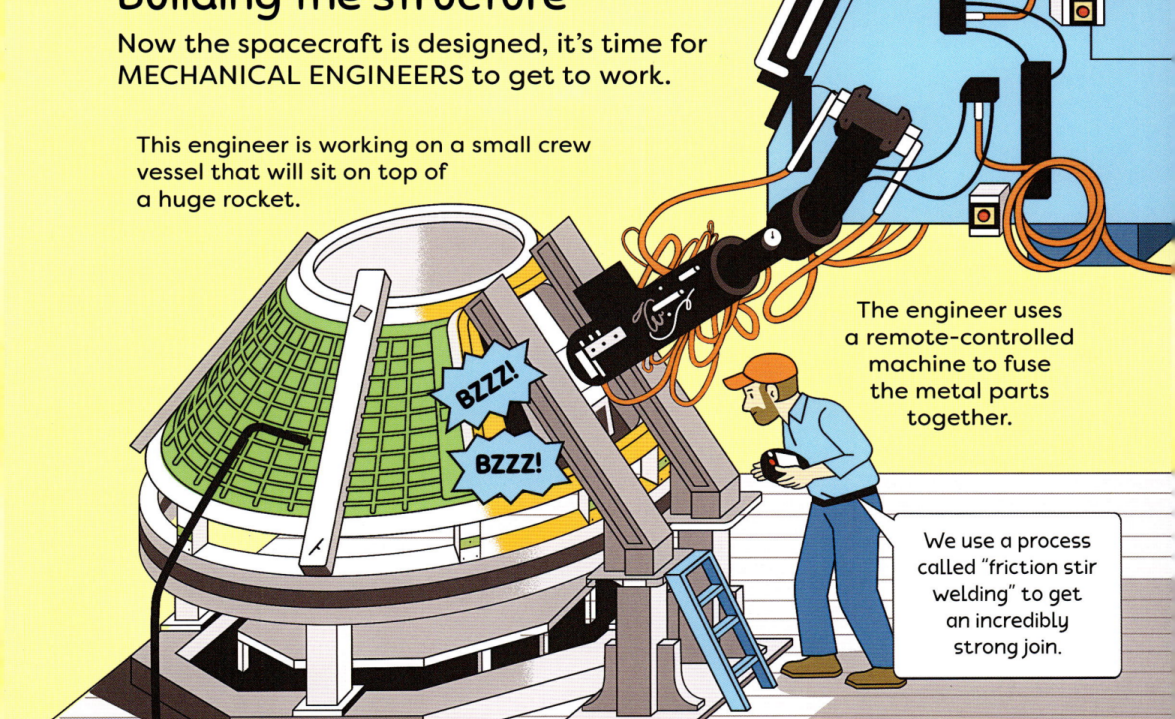

The structure is built in an **assembly factory.** NASA's factory in New Orleans, USA, is one of the largest buildings in the WORLD – around the size of 30 football fields.

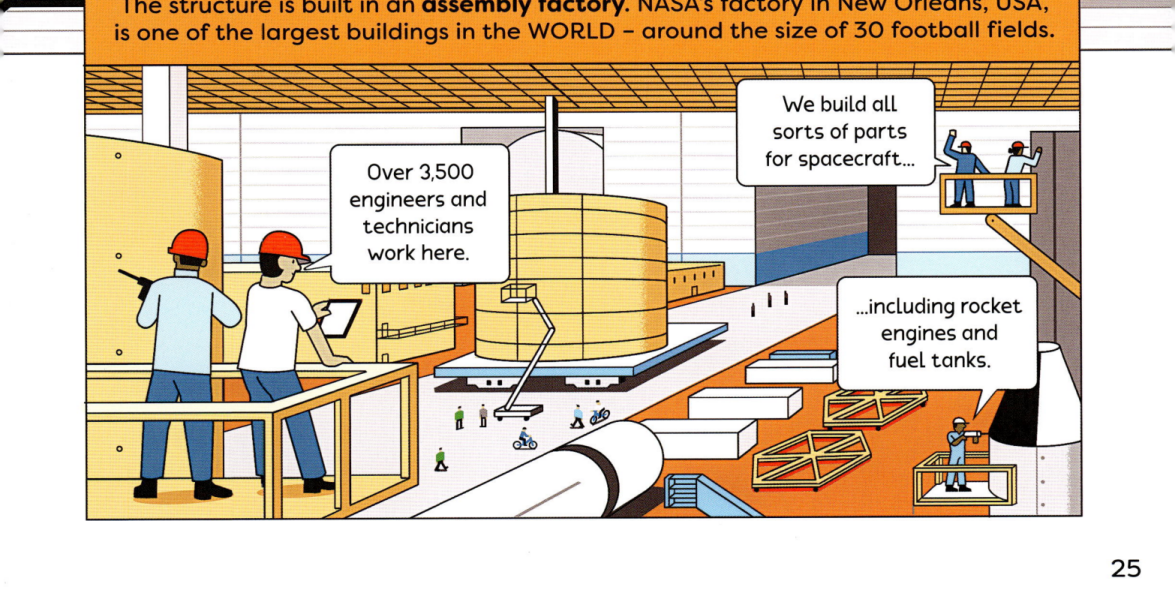

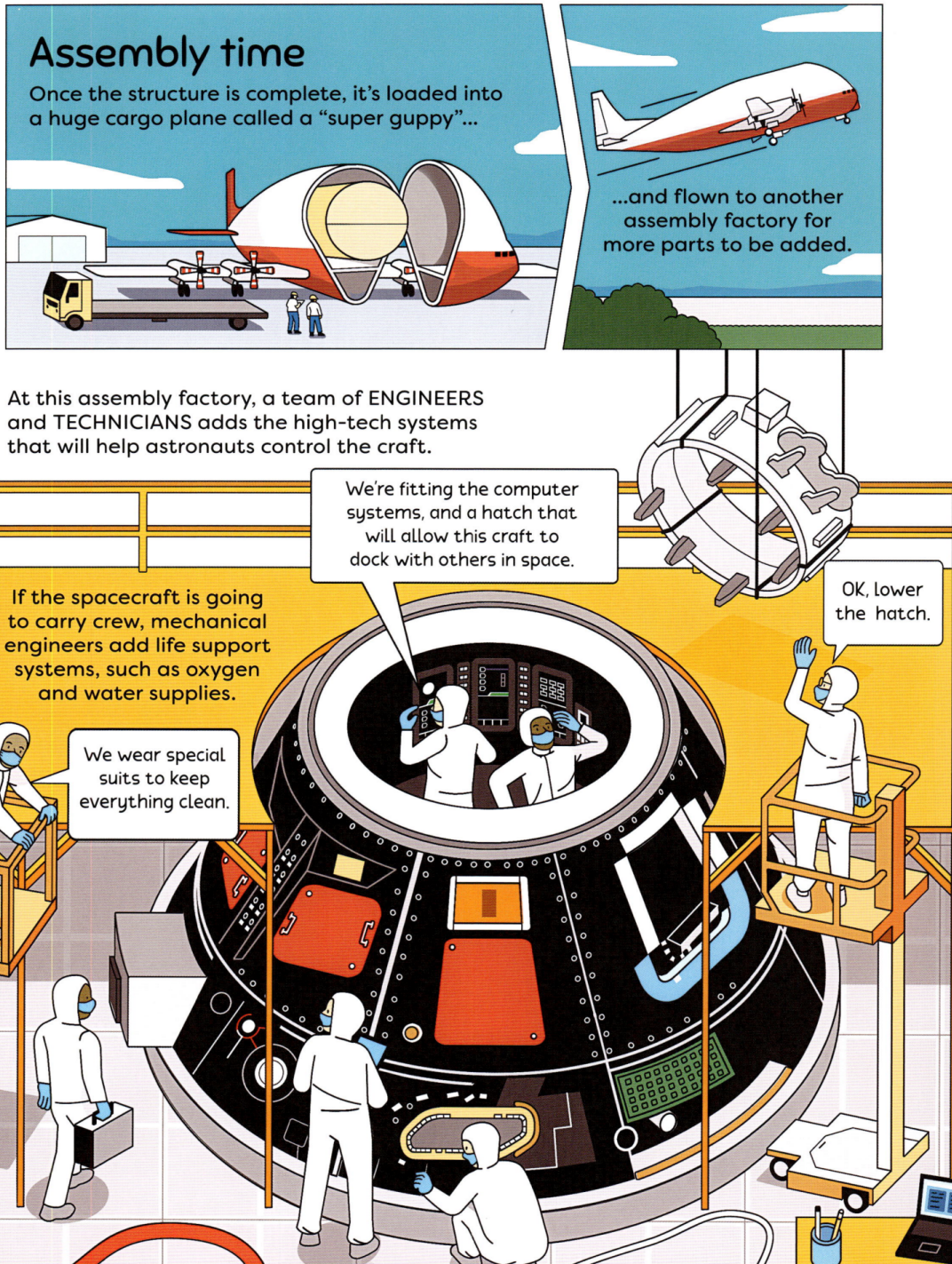

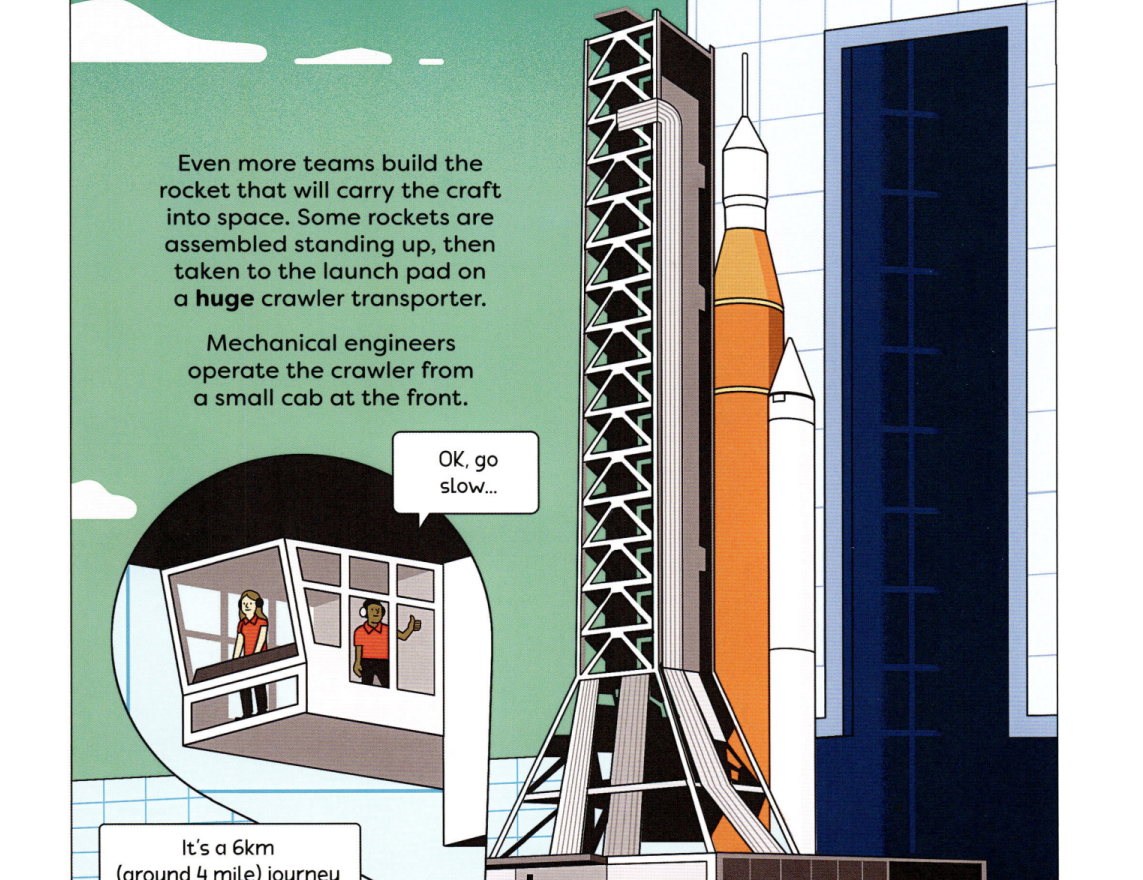

Space simulation

To test a spacecraft REALLY thoroughly, test engineers recreate the effects of space in a chamber known as a **space simulator**. Engineers wear special suits, so they don't contaminate the chamber.

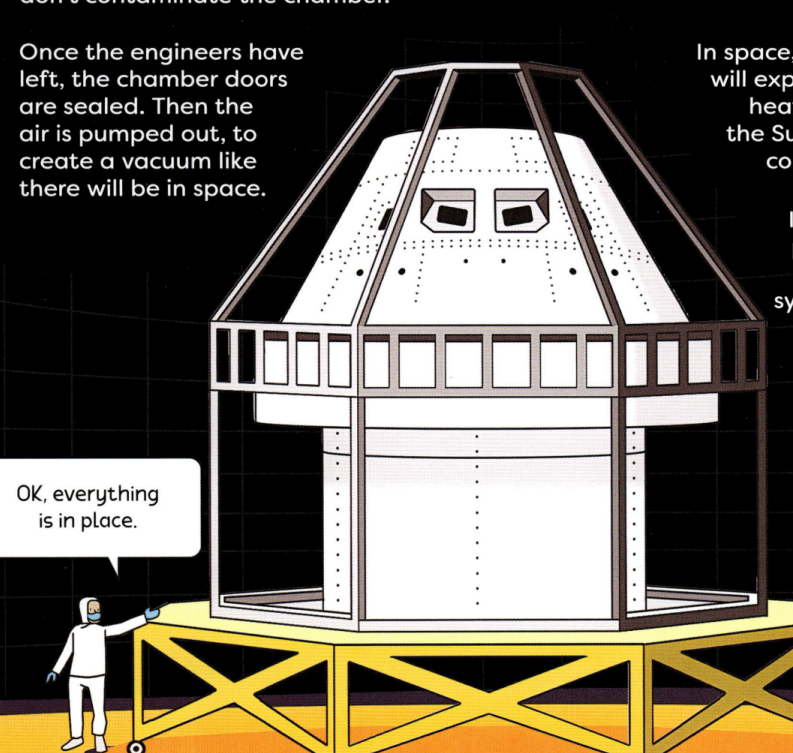

Once the engineers have left, the chamber doors are sealed. Then the air is pumped out, to create a vacuum like there will be in space.

In space, the spacecraft will experience blazing heat when it's lit by the Sun, and freezing cold when it's not.

In the chamber, powerful lamps and cooling systems recreate these extreme temperatures.

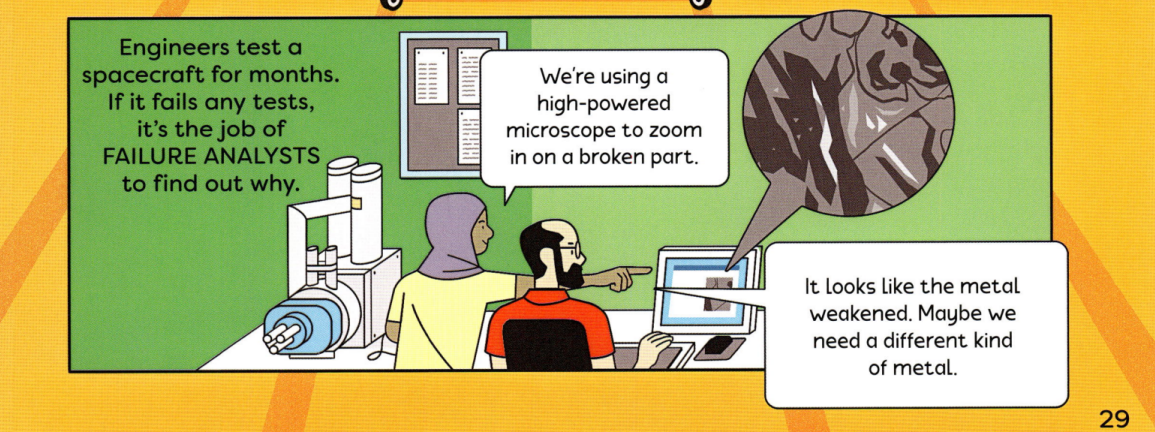

Engineers test a spacecraft for months. If it fails any tests, it's the job of FAILURE ANALYSTS to find out why.

Up, up and away!

Training is over and the spacecraft is ready. At last it's time for your mission. Behind the scenes, a huge team of experts works hard to make sure the launch goes smoothly...

LAUNCH TECHNICIANS check the spacecraft is ready for launch.

SUIT TECHNICIANS help astronauts with their flight suits.

FUEL TECHNICIANS load the rocket with fuel.

LAUNCH CONTROLLERS oversee the first crucial minutes of the spacecraft's launch.

FLIGHT CONTROLLERS are in charge of the spacecraft's flight into space and back to Earth.

The countdown begins

The day is finally here – soon, the astronauts will blast off into space. Behind the scenes, a team of LAUNCH TECHNICIANS and engineers works hard to make sure the launch goes smoothly...

24 hours to launch

The rocket is carried from its assembly building to the launch site on a long transporter vehicle.

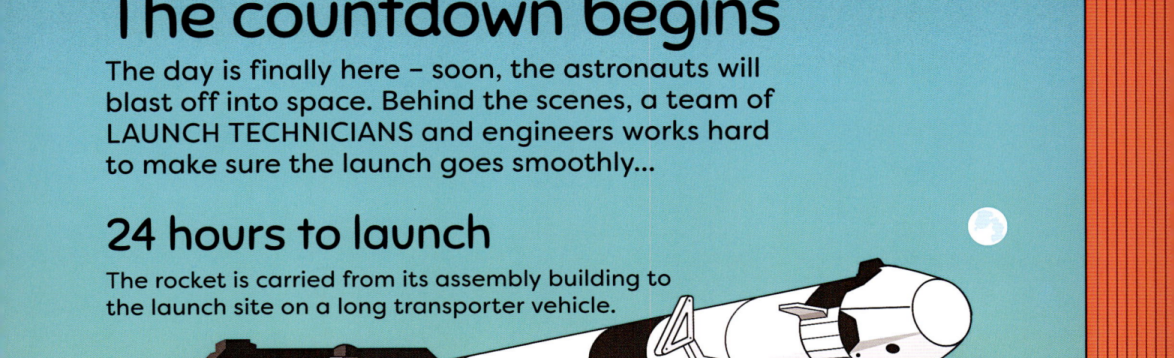

The rocket is **very** heavy, so the transporter drives **very** slowly, with engineers guiding it the whole way.

10 hours

At the launch site, the transporter raises the rocket up... and up... into its launch position.

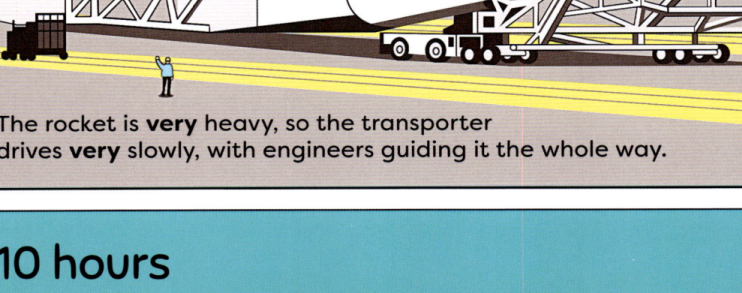

Launch technicians and mechanical engineers inspect the launch pad to make sure all the equipment is in place.

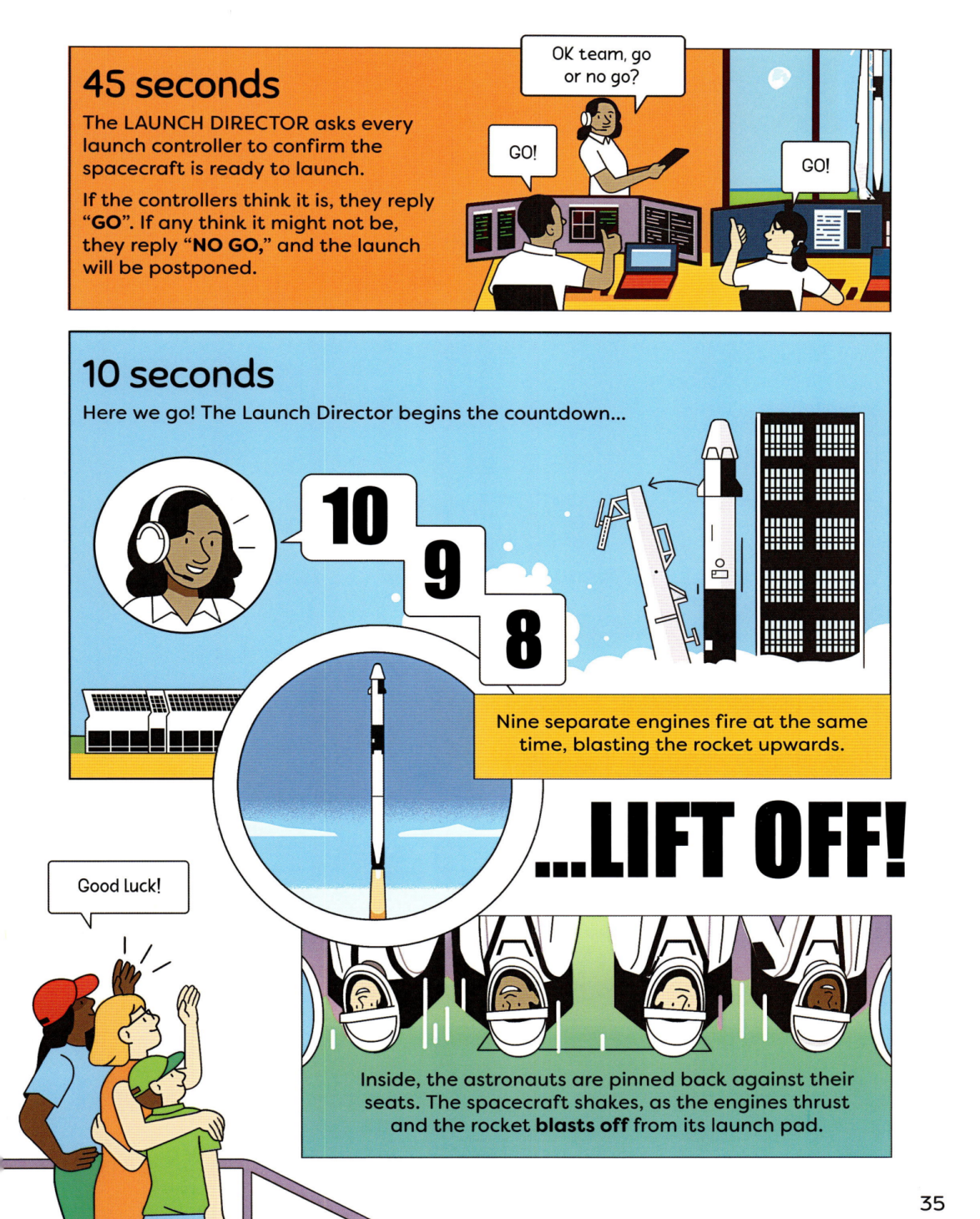

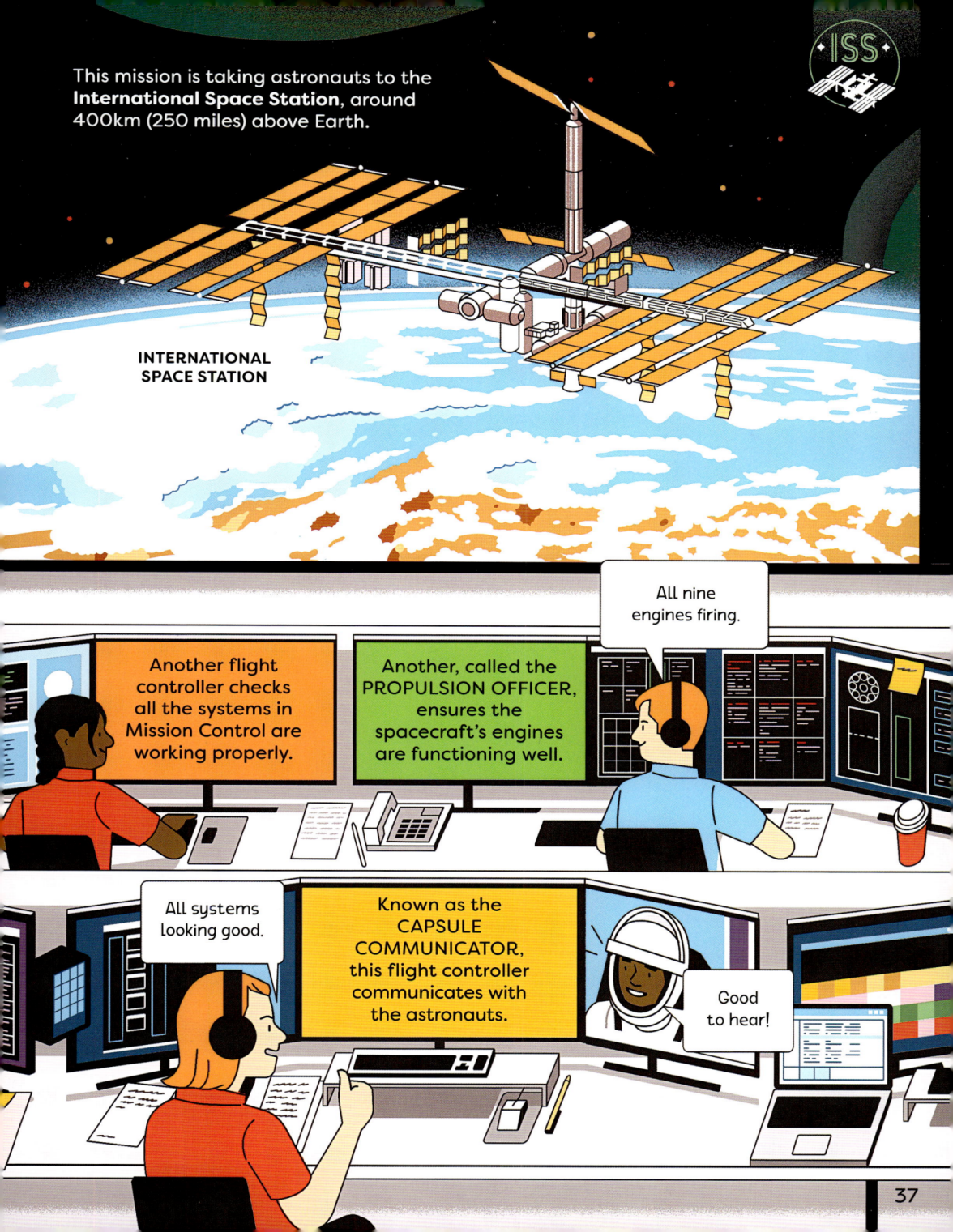

To the space station

Just 70 seconds after lift-off, the rocket is rising faster than the **speed of sound.** Flight controllers monitor every moment...

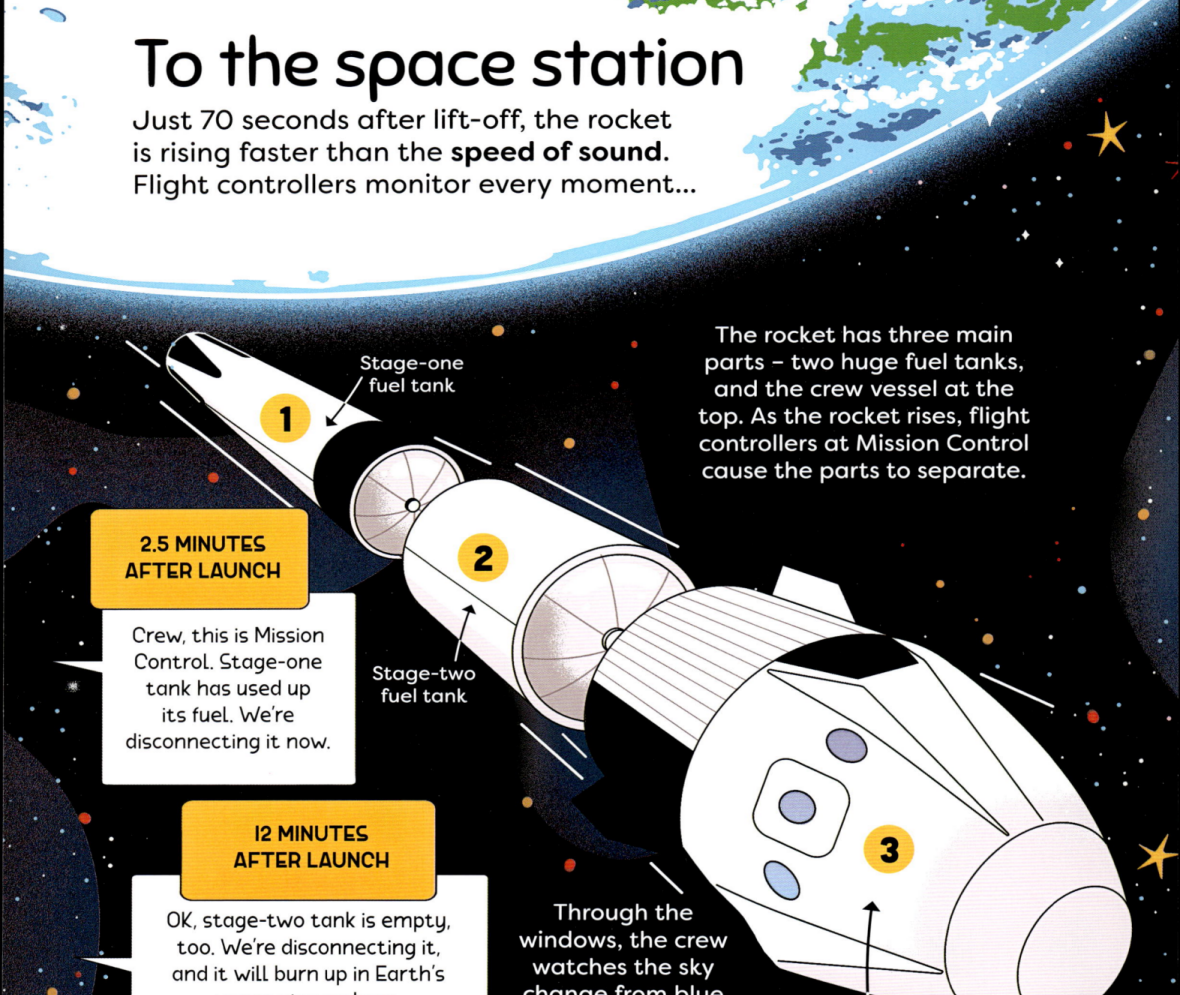

The rocket has three main parts – two huge fuel tanks, and the crew vessel at the top. As the rocket rises, flight controllers at Mission Control cause the parts to separate.

2.5 MINUTES AFTER LAUNCH

Crew, this is Mission Control. Stage-one tank has used up its fuel. We're disconnecting it now.

12 MINUTES AFTER LAUNCH

OK, stage-two tank is empty, too. We're disconnecting it, and it will burn up in Earth's upper atmosphere.

Through the windows, the crew watches the sky change from blue to deep black.

As the stage-one tank falls, it flips around. Landing legs extend from the sides, and an engine fires to slow it down to land.

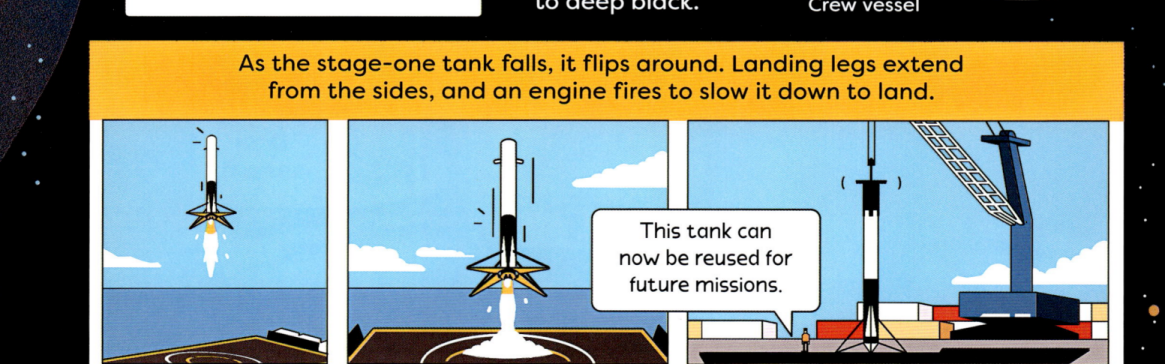

This tank can now be reused for future missions.

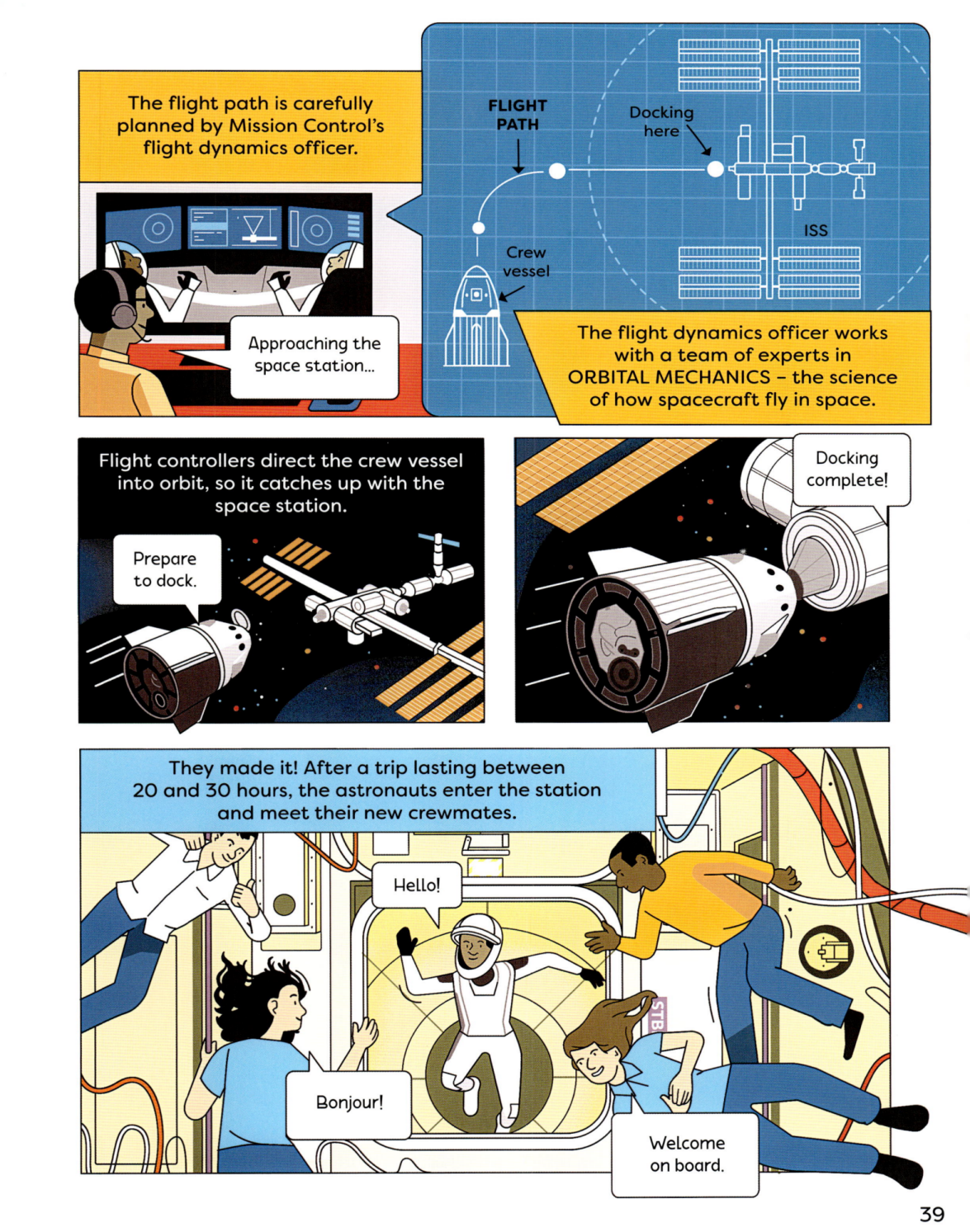

Do you want to help run a space station?

It takes lots of different experts on Earth to keep astronauts safe, healthy and comfortable in space.

FLIGHT CONTROLLERS make sure the space station is working properly and its crew are safe.

FOOD SCIENTISTS plan and pack astronauts' meals.

BIOMEDICAL OFFICERS make sure astronauts stay healthy.

EVA OFFICERS plan and oversee spacewalks.

SPACESUIT DESIGNERS create the spacesuits that astronauts wear on spacewalks.

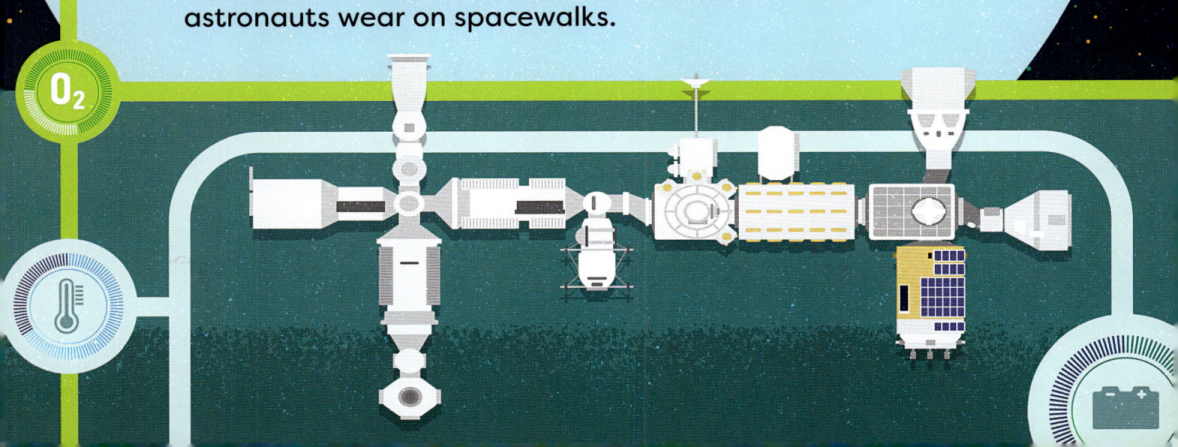

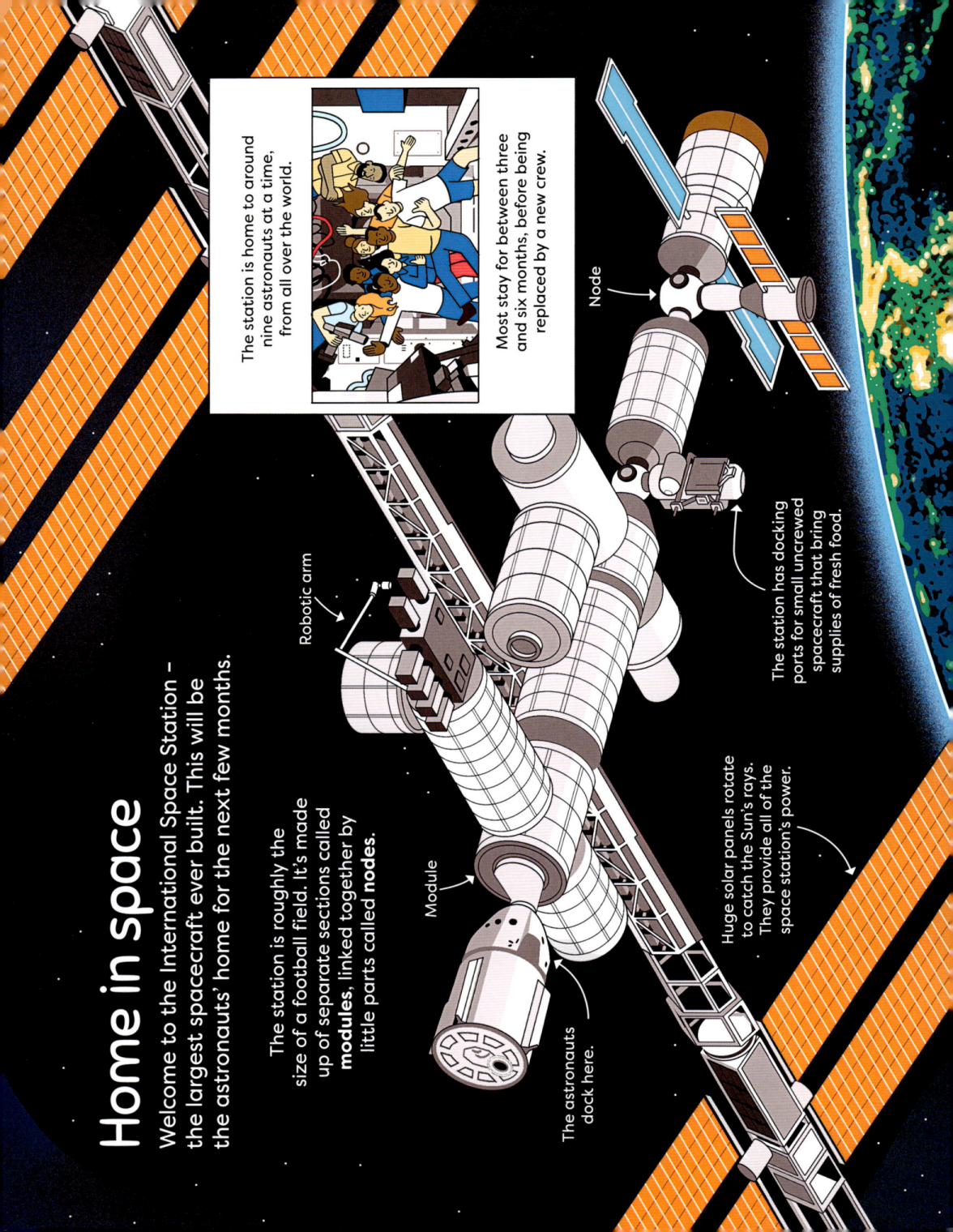

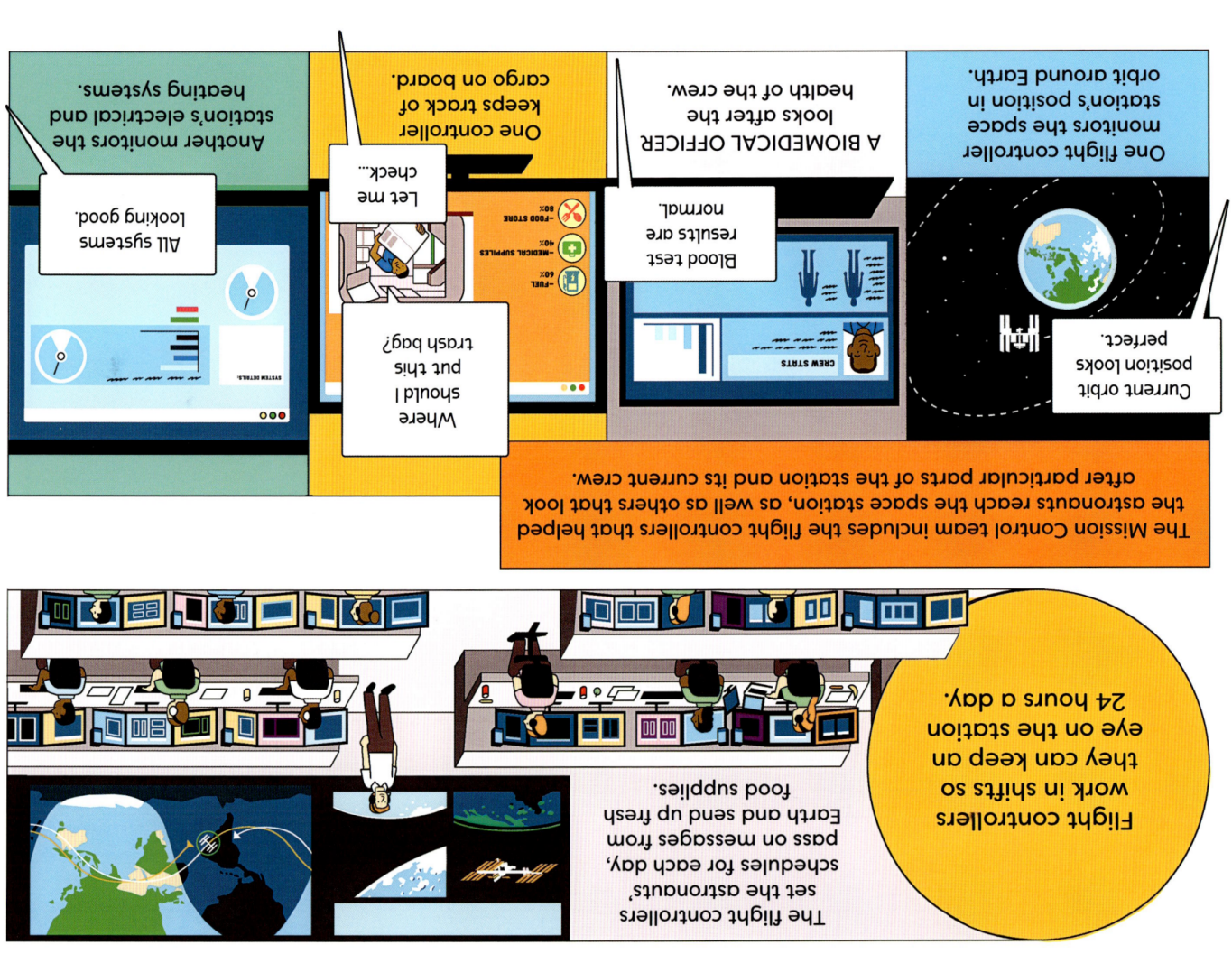

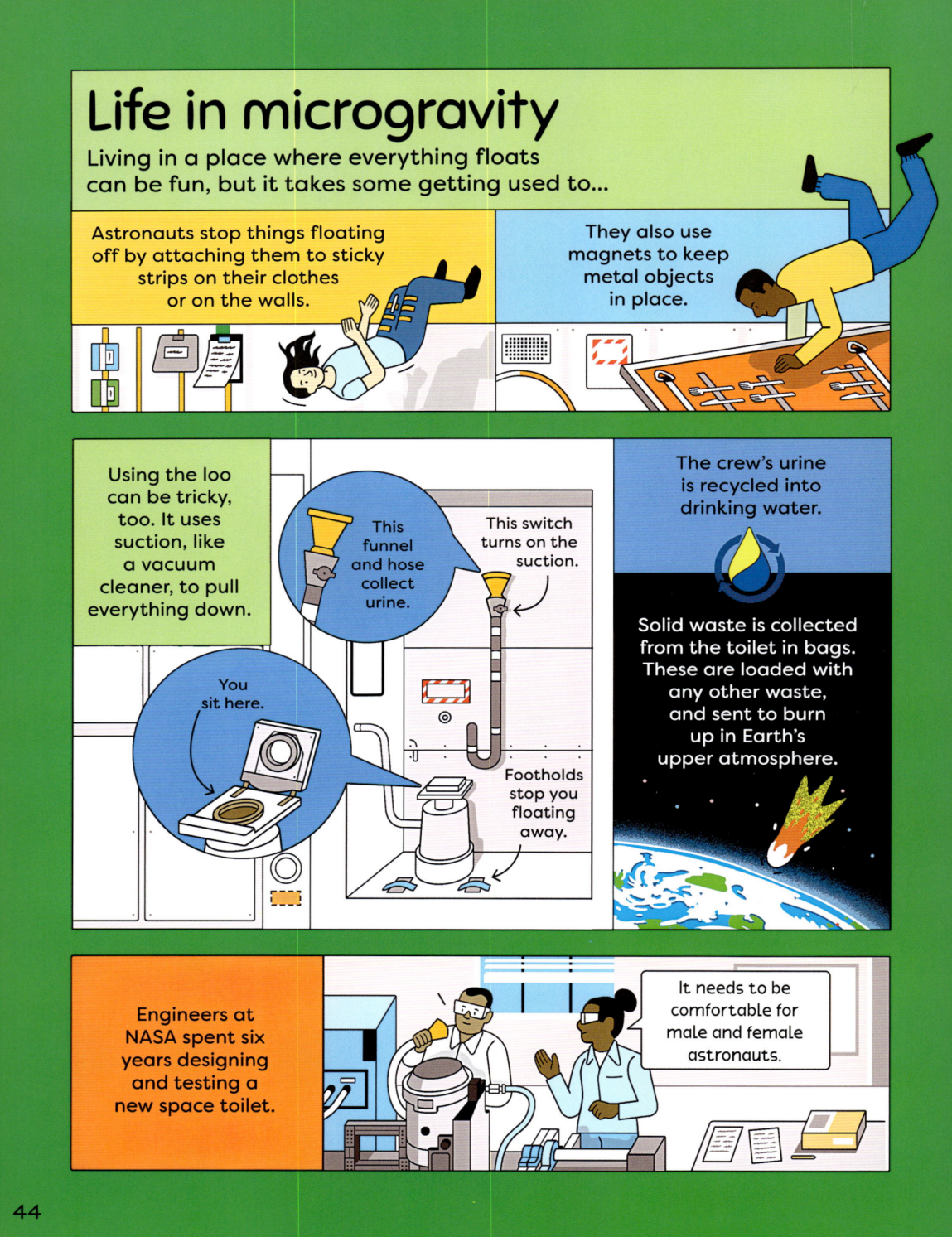

Living in microgravity for a long time can affect your body.

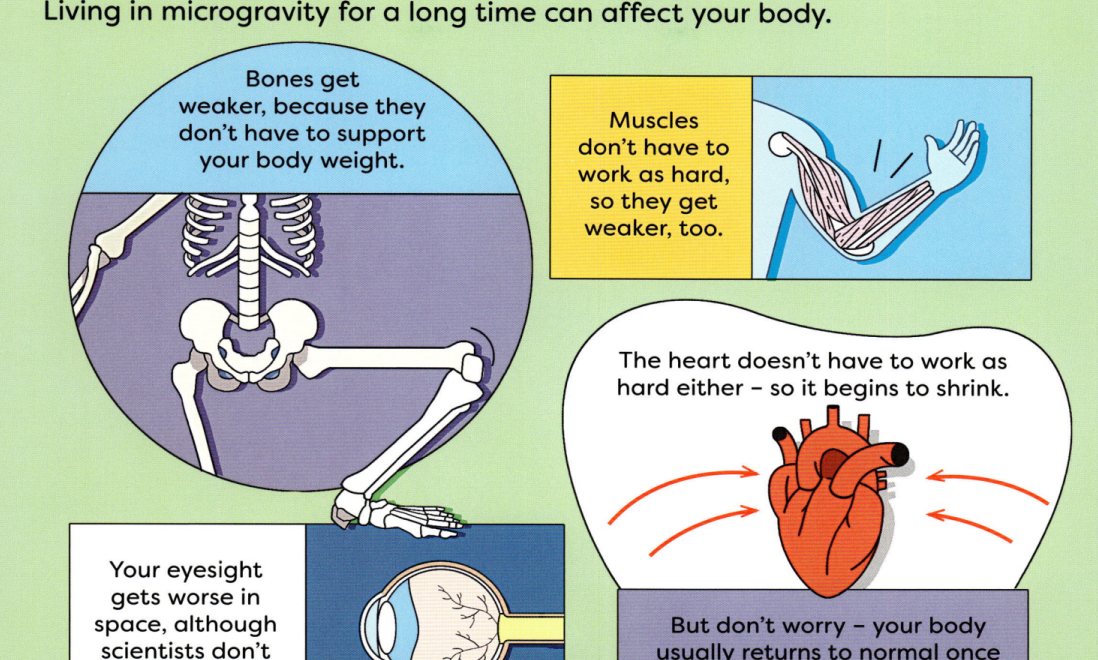

But don't worry – your body usually returns to normal once you're back on Earth.

Working out

To stay strong, astronauts exercise for at least two hours a day. The space station has specially adapted exercise machines, with straps.

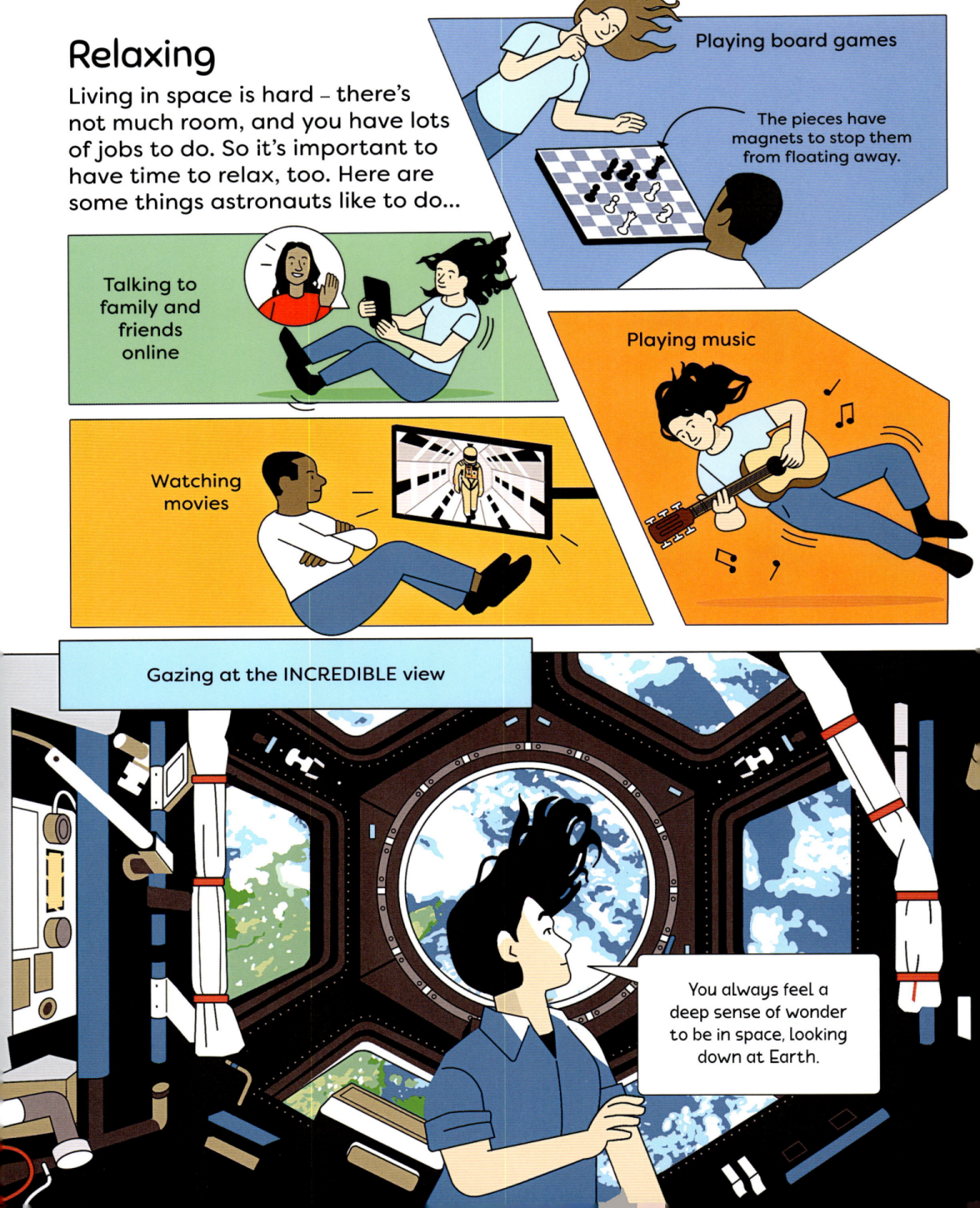

Washing

In microgravity, water doesn't flow as it does on Earth. If you ran a shower, bubbles of water would float all over the place. But you can still keep clean.

To brush their teeth, they squeeze a blob of water from a pouch and catch it in their mouth. They add toothpaste, then brush with their mouth closed and spit the foam into a paper towel.

Sleeping

Astronauts each have their own **sleep station** – a private cubicle with a sleeping bag strapped to the wall.

They don't need a pillow. They just sleep floating in the bag.

The station's lights and noisy air pumps can make it hard to sleep. So most astronauts wear sleep masks and ear plugs.

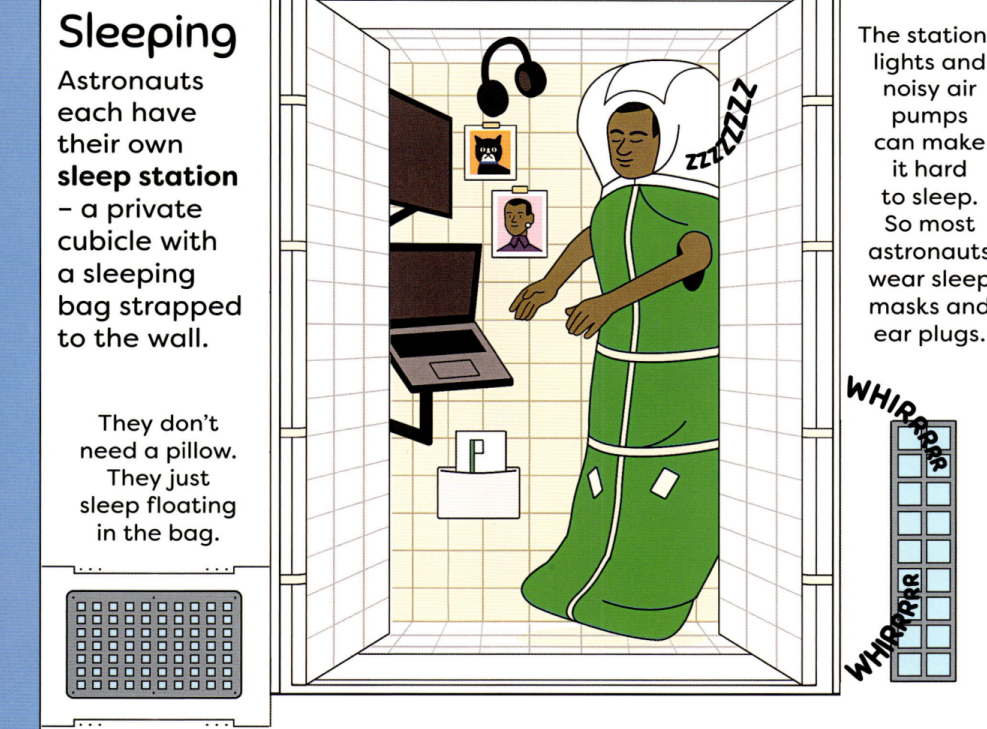

Spacewalking

A **spacewalk** – when you put on a spacesuit and leave the safety of your craft – is one of the hardest tasks. It requires months of planning, starting long before you leave Earth.

Advance planning

Every spacewalk – officially known as an extra vehicular activity, or EVA – is planned and controlled by an EVA OFFICER. The EVA officer meets the astronauts and talks them through every detail of what they will need to do.

Suit development

With extreme temperatures and no air, space is a dangerous place. The suits astronauts wear for spacewalks are carefully built by spacesuit designers.

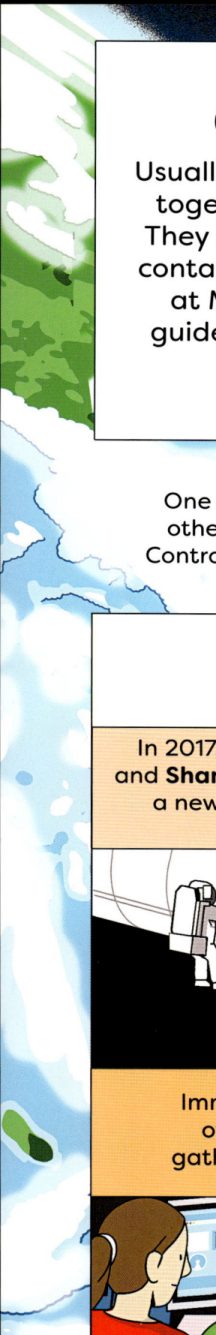

On the day

Usually, two astronauts work together on a spacewalk. They stay in constant radio contact with the EVA officer at Mission Control, who guides them through their different tasks.

One suit has red bands while the other doesn't. This helps Mission Control to tell the astronauts apart.

Long safety lines or **tethers** connect the astronauts to the station.

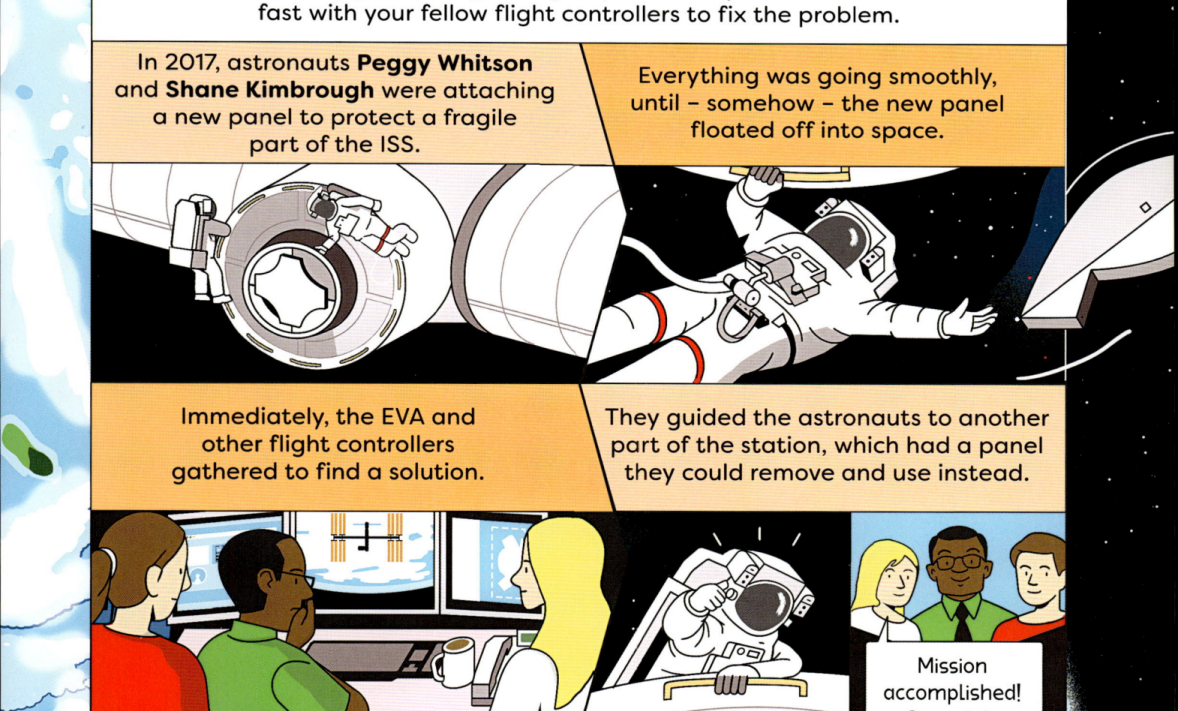

To be an EVA officer, you need a cool head in emergencies. If anything goes wrong during a spacewalk, you'll have to work fast with your fellow flight controllers to fix the problem.

In 2017, astronauts **Peggy Whitson** and **Shane Kimbrough** were attaching a new panel to protect a fragile part of the ISS.

Everything was going smoothly, until – somehow – the new panel floated off into space.

Immediately, the EVA and other flight controllers gathered to find a solution.

They guided the astronauts to another part of the station, which had a panel they could remove and use instead.

Mission accomplished! Great job.

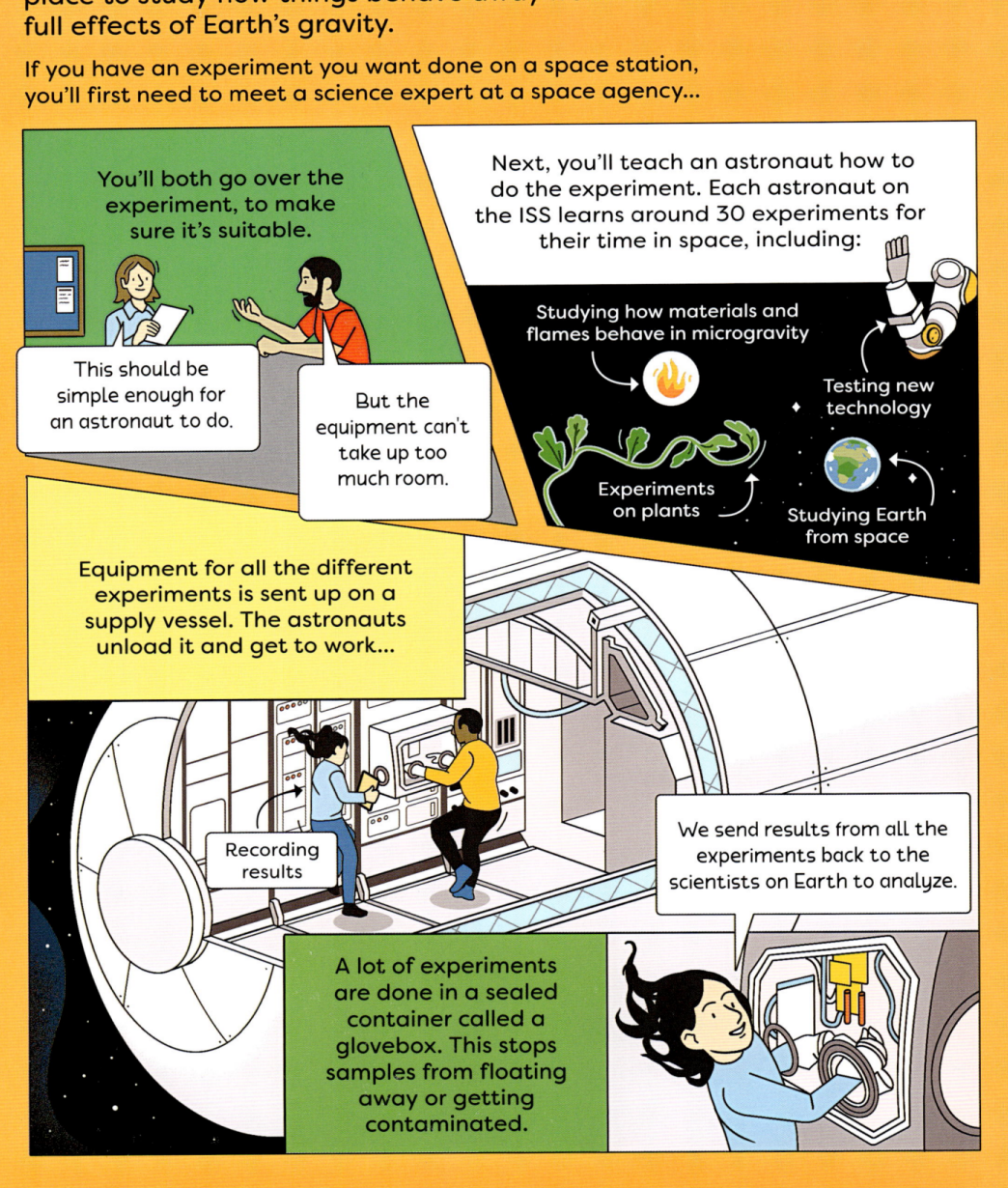

Biomedical scientists use space to study living human cells. Devices called **tissue chips** are specially designed to grow cells in space.

In microgravity, cells form more complex 3D structures than on Earth. This makes it easier to see how the cells react to different drugs.

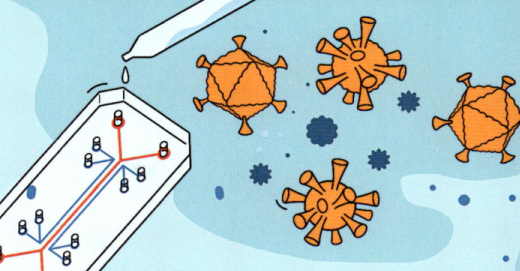

Astronauts also carry out experiments on themselves. Scientists think that changes to the astronauts' bodies in space may be similar to the effects of ageing on Earth.

They measure the shape of their eyes using an instrument called a **fundoscope**.

Astronauts take urine and blood samples to send home.

By studying changes in astronauts, scientists hope to help people on Earth live longer, healthier lives.

The twins experiment

In 2017, US astronaut **Scott Kelly** spent 340 days on board the ISS, while his identical twin **Mark** remained on Earth.

Each brother took the same regular tests, including cell samples, and played games to test their memory and reaction speed.

Scott's body experienced changes that Mark's didn't – including in his cells and how his brain worked.

The study raised questions over the safety of long-term space travel for humans.

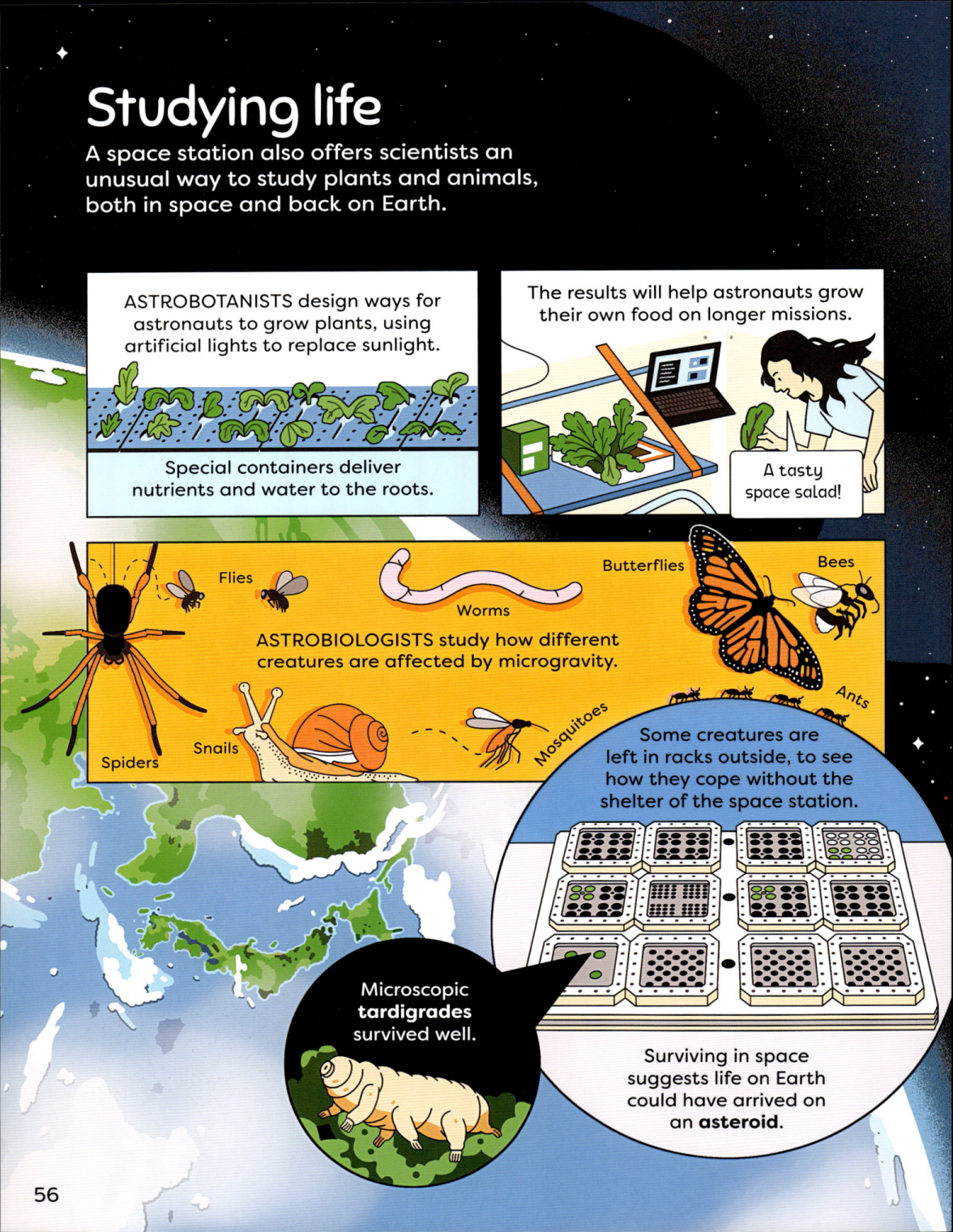

An eye on Earth

EARTH SCIENTISTS use hi-tech cameras mounted on the space station to monitor the health of our planet.

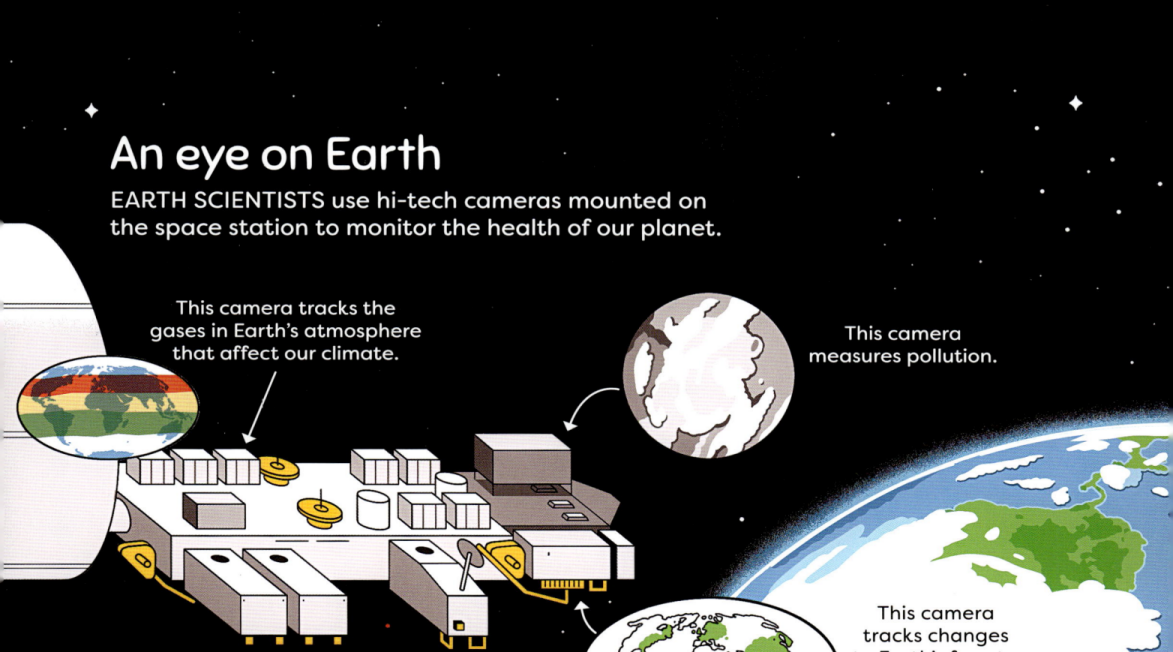

Say cheese...

The ISS is close enough to Earth for its crew to snap amazingly detailed photos. The images go online, for anyone to study.

Space tech

If you're into technology, then a space station is an exciting place, where cutting-edge inventions, especially in robotics, are tested for missions even **deeper** into space.

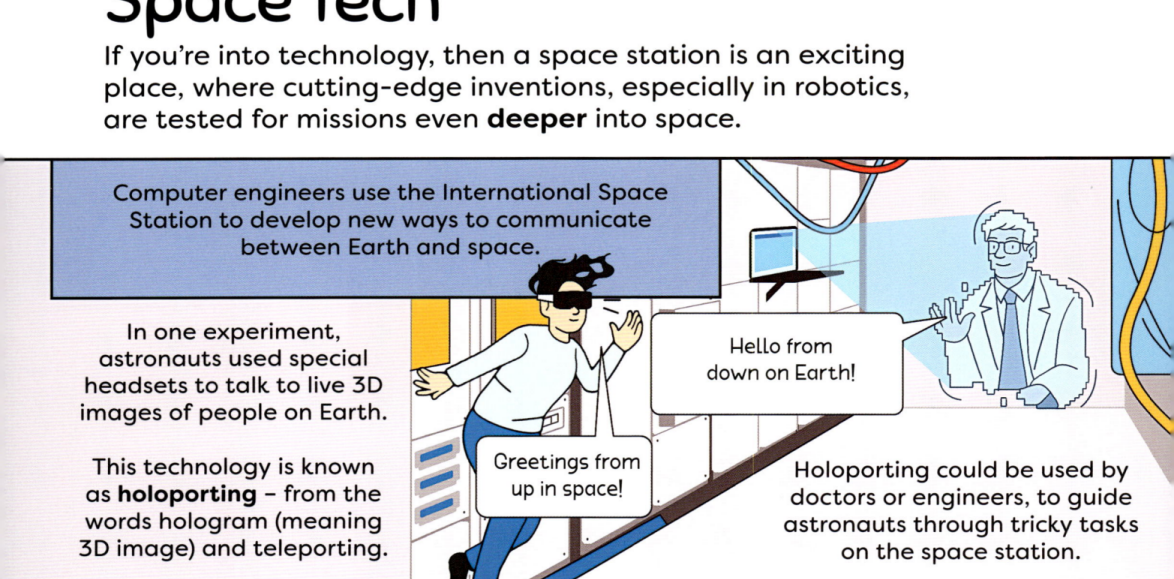

Computer engineers use the International Space Station to develop new ways to communicate between Earth and space.

In one experiment, astronauts used special headsets to talk to live 3D images of people on Earth.

This technology is known as **holoporting** – from the words hologram (meaning 3D image) and teleporting.

Holoporting could be used by doctors or engineers, to guide astronauts through tricky tasks on the space station.

Busy bees

Watch out – there's a flying robot around! In another experiment, ROBOTICS ENGINEERS tested flying robots called **Astrobees**.

Astrobees use cameras and remote sensors to find their way around.

They have electric fans to push themselves along.

In the future, Astrobees could look after spacecraft on very long missions, while the crew are put into a deep sleep.

Robonaut

Engineers also tested a high-tech humanoid robot called **Robonaut**.

To operate Robonaut, astronauts put on a headset and wrist attachments.

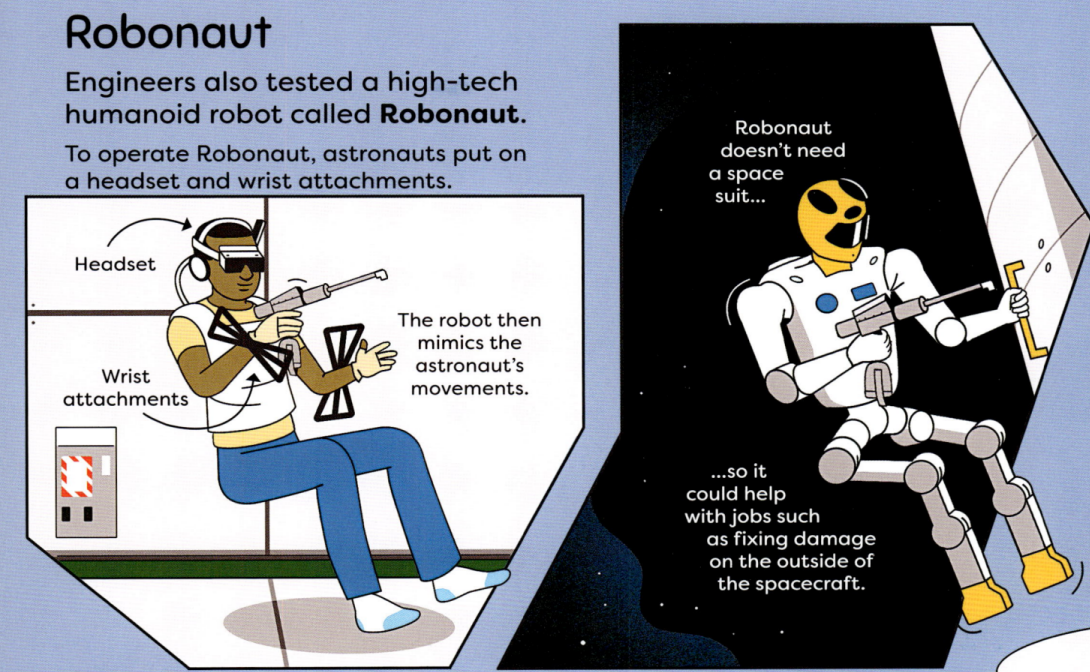

Hi-tech workers

Engineers are designing even more hi-tech robots to send on future space missions.

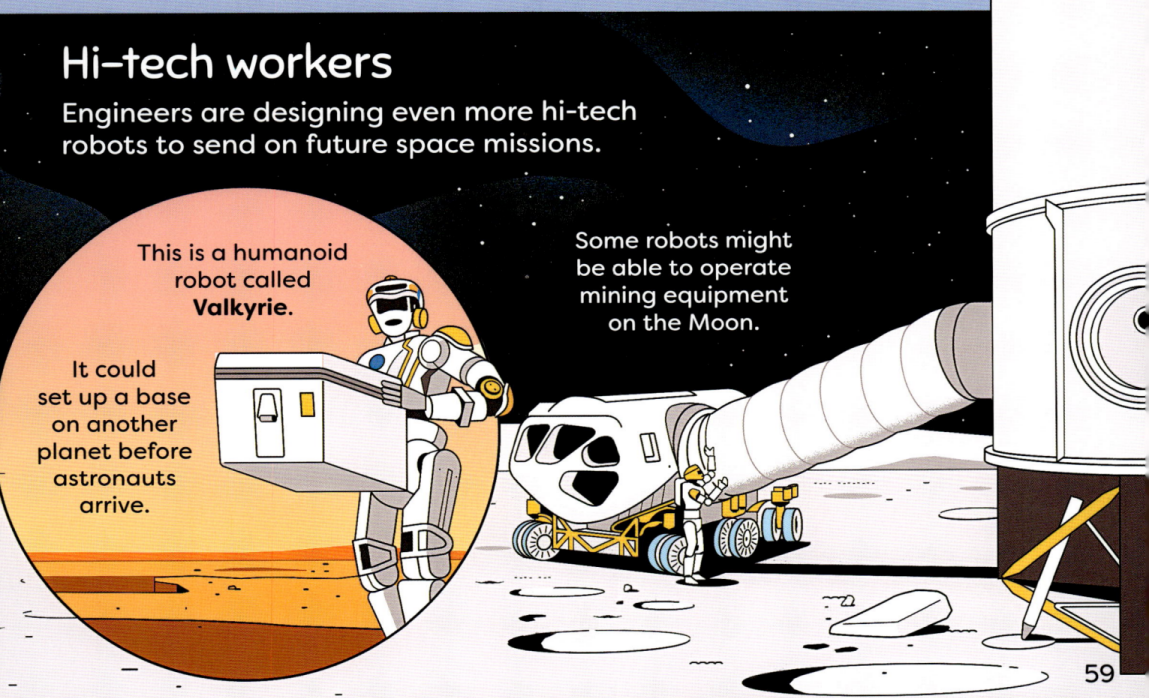

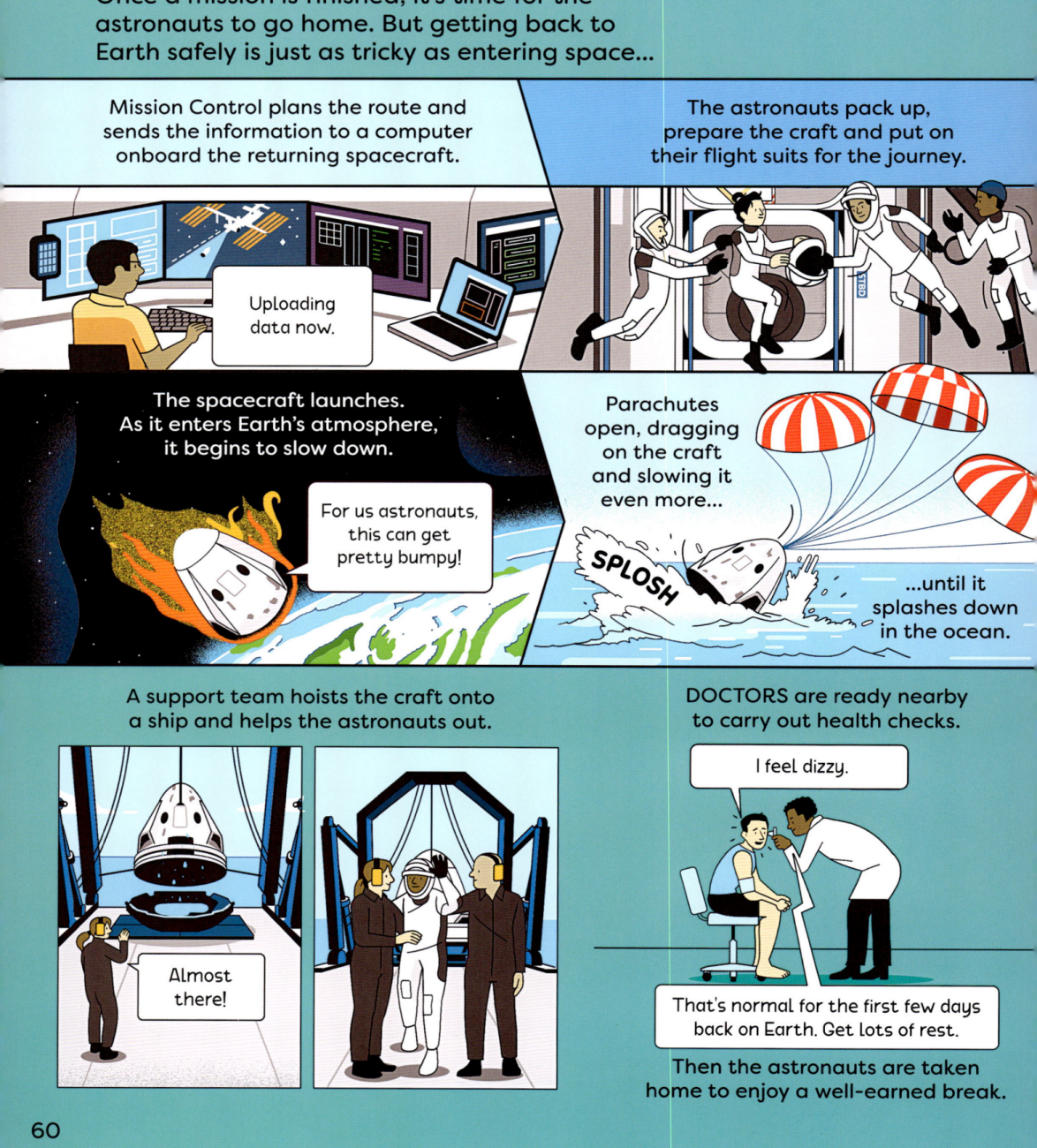

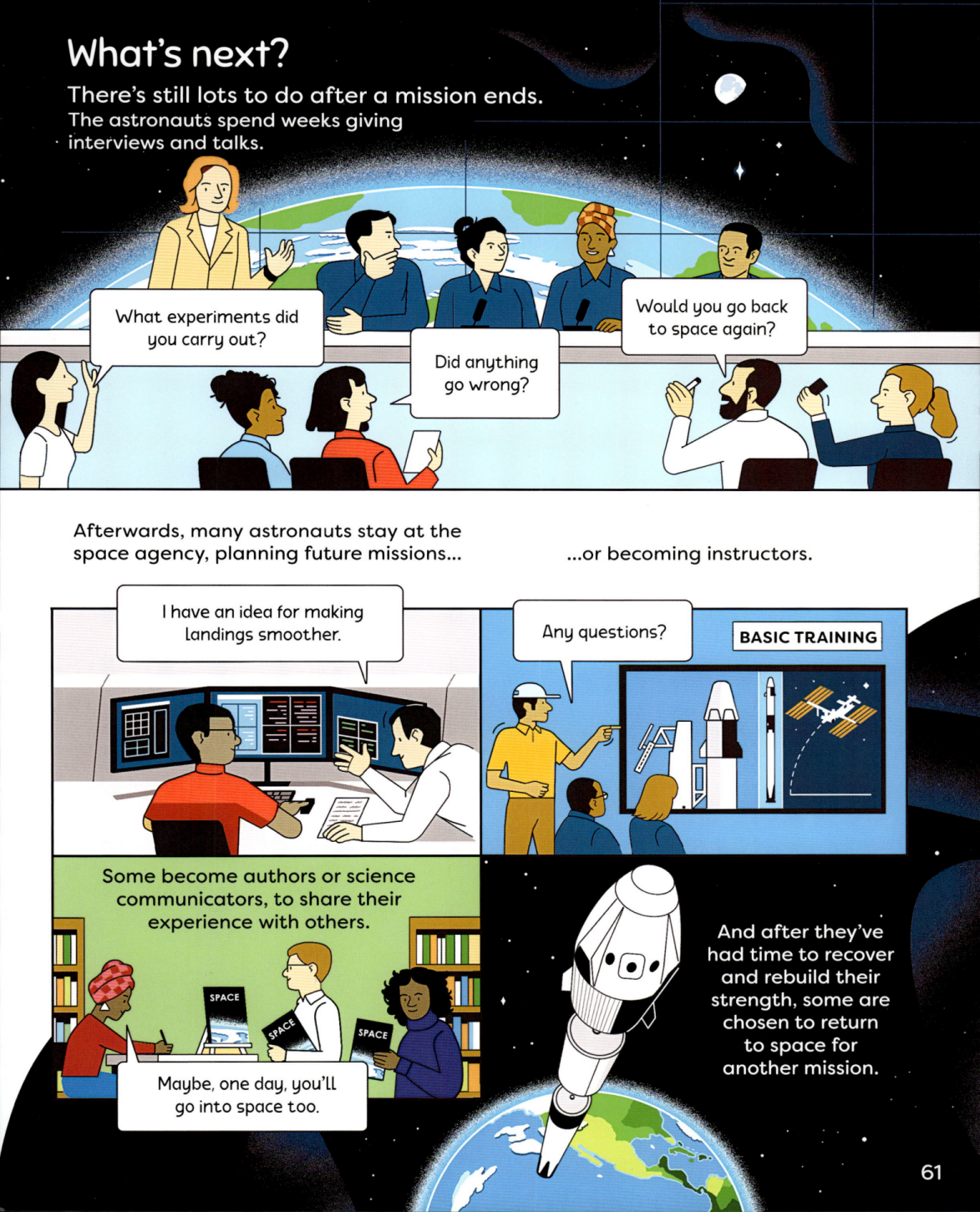

Exploring further

Do you dream of living on the Moon or visiting alien planets? Lots of people are working to bring that dream closer to reality...

ASTRONOMERS study stars, planets, moons and everything else in space.

NAVIGATORS control probes as they travel through space.

ARTIFICIAL INTELLIGENCE (AI) ENGINEERS program robotic rovers to explore alien environments on their own.

SPACE ARCHITECTS design future space habitats.

PSYCHOLOGISTS study how living on another planet might affect people's mental health.

Moon missions

It has been over 50 years since humans first landed on the Moon. Now, several space agencies are working together on a new Moon exploration program.

Aerospace engineers are planning the first ever **lunar base camp** – a place for crews to stay on the Moon.

Here's what it could look like...

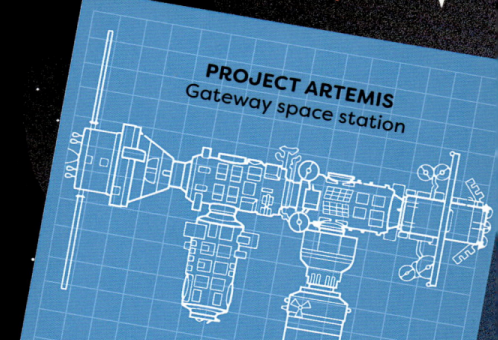

PROJECT ARTEMIS Gateway space station

They have also designed a space station that will orbit the Moon for at least a decade.

In the future, crews might stop here before heading to Mars.

LUNAR BASE CAMP

Space elevator to transport astronauts and supplies to and from spacecraft.

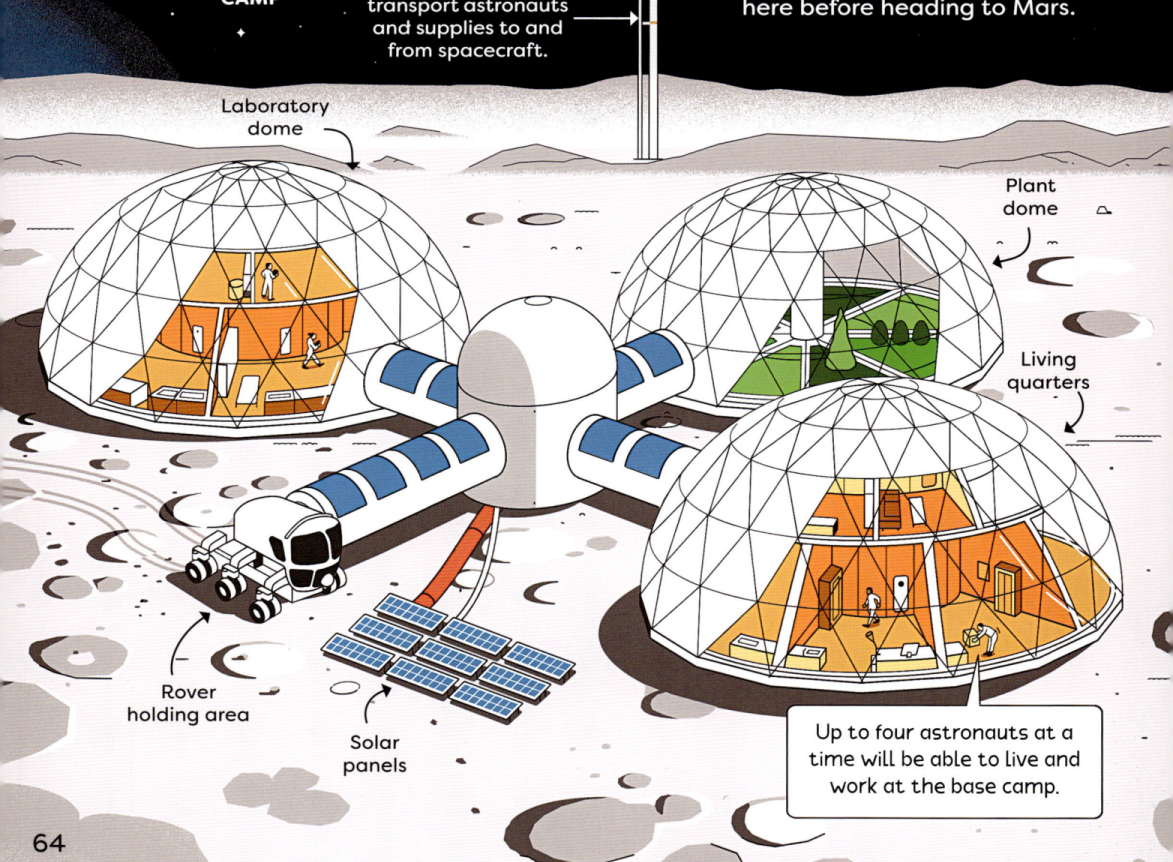

Up to four astronauts at a time will be able to live and work at the base camp.

Lunar training

Some astronauts are preparing for future missions at the Desert Research and Technology Studies center – Desert RATS for short – in Arizona, USA.

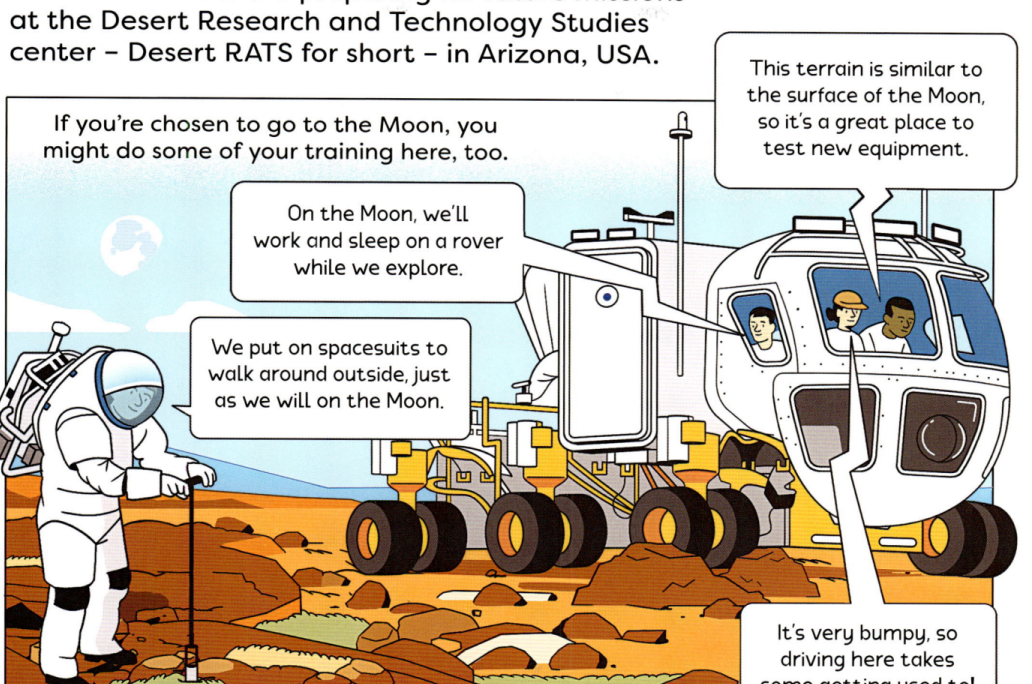

Red planet rovers

Of all the planets in our Solar System, Mars is the one most like Earth. ROBOTICS ENGINEERS have sent rovers to study Mars – paving the way for future visits by astronauts.

Mars rovers collect information and send data back to Earth. But creating devices that can cope with Mars is tricky...

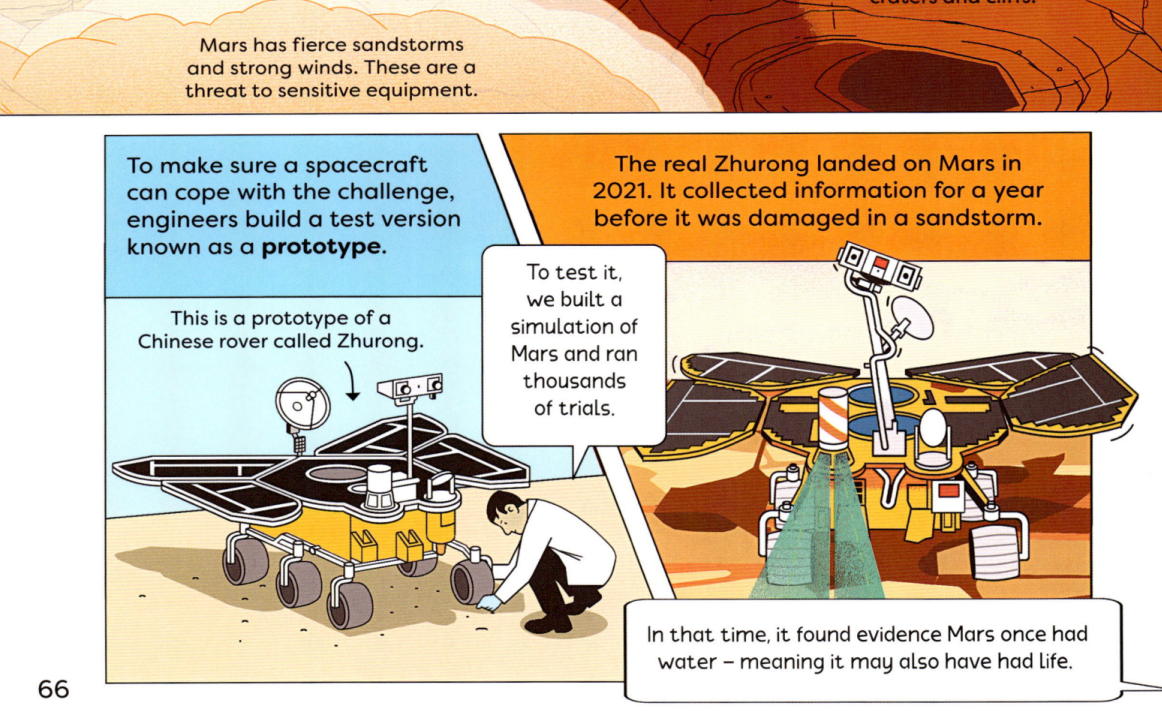

High-tech team

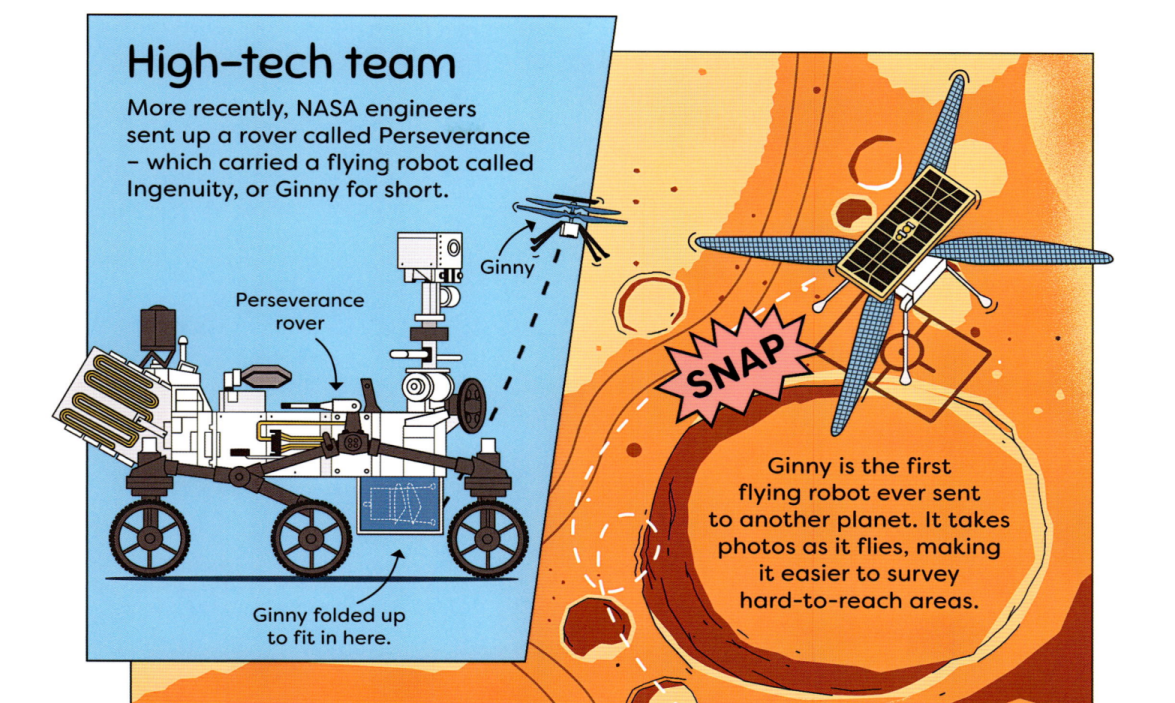

More recently, NASA engineers sent up a rover called Perseverance – which carried a flying robot called Ingenuity, or Ginny for short.

Ginny is the first flying robot ever sent to another planet. It takes photos as it flies, making it easier to survey hard-to-reach areas.

Perseverance is collecting lots of information for scientists. One of its main tasks is searching rocks for any chemical clues that tiny organisms once lived on Mars.

ARTIFICIAL INTELLIGENCE (AI) ENGINEERS are working on computer programs that could allow rovers to make their own decisions about where to go and what to do.

To help train the programs to recognize different types of terrain, they built a website which anyone could visit. The website showed photos taken by rovers, and asked people to add labels to different areas.

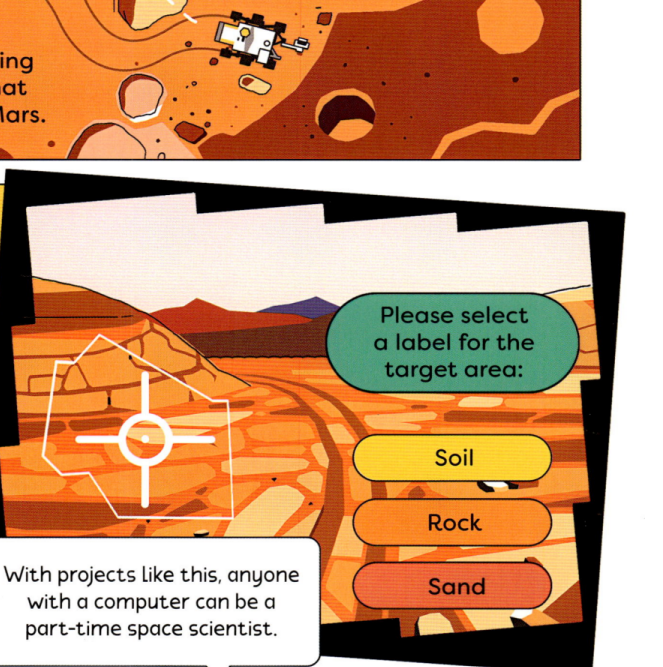

With projects like this, anyone with a computer can be a part-time space scientist.

Destination: Mars

The race is on to land the first humans on Mars. This won't be possible without powerful new technology and equipment. If you like a challenge, this could be the area for you.

With current rocket technology, NASA estimates it would take nine months for astronauts to reach Mars.

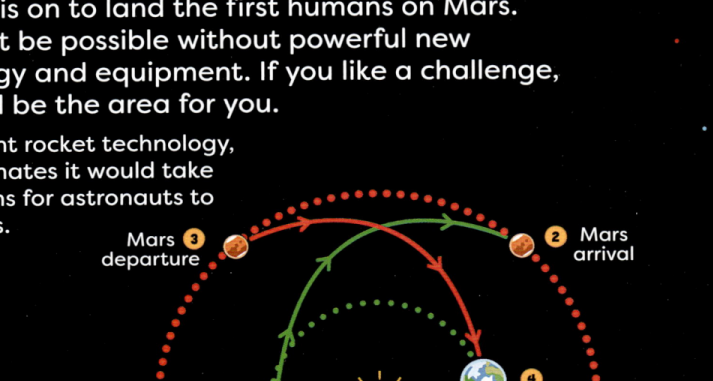

— Earth to Mars (235 days)
— Mars to Earth (191 days)
• • Earth orbit around the Sun
• • Mars orbit around the Sun

To get there AND back would take nearly two years, as crews would need to wait months for Earth and Mars to move into the right positions for a return journey.

Engineers are working to find ways to make the journey quicker and more efficient. Some are investigating different types of fuel.

We're working on a method called **nuclear propulsion**. Instead of burning fuel, it uses energy from atoms – the tiny particles which make up everything.

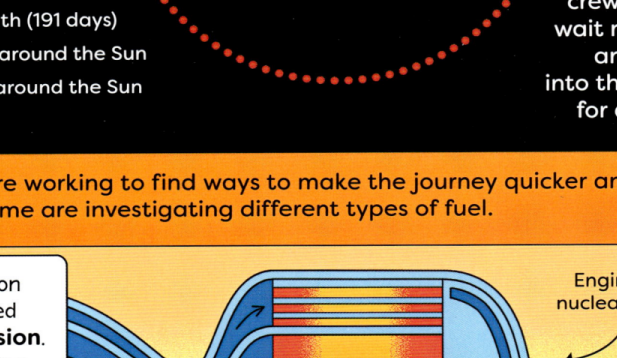

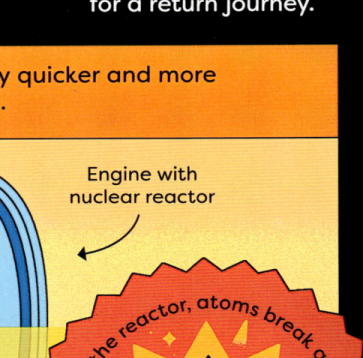

Engine with nuclear reactor

Inside the reactor, atoms break apart... ...and release vast amounts of energy.

If we can perfect the technology, it will give rockets much **more** push using much **less** fuel.

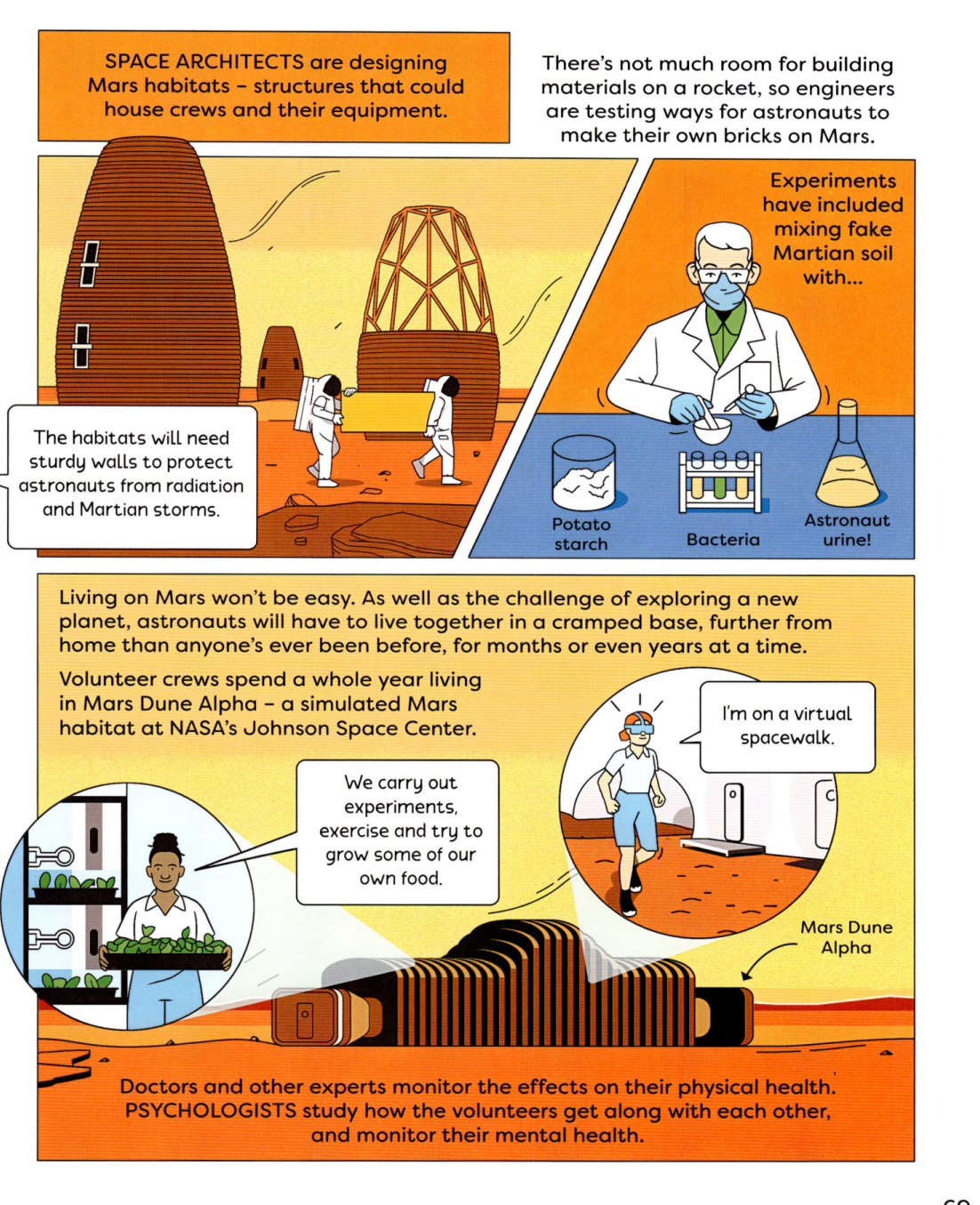

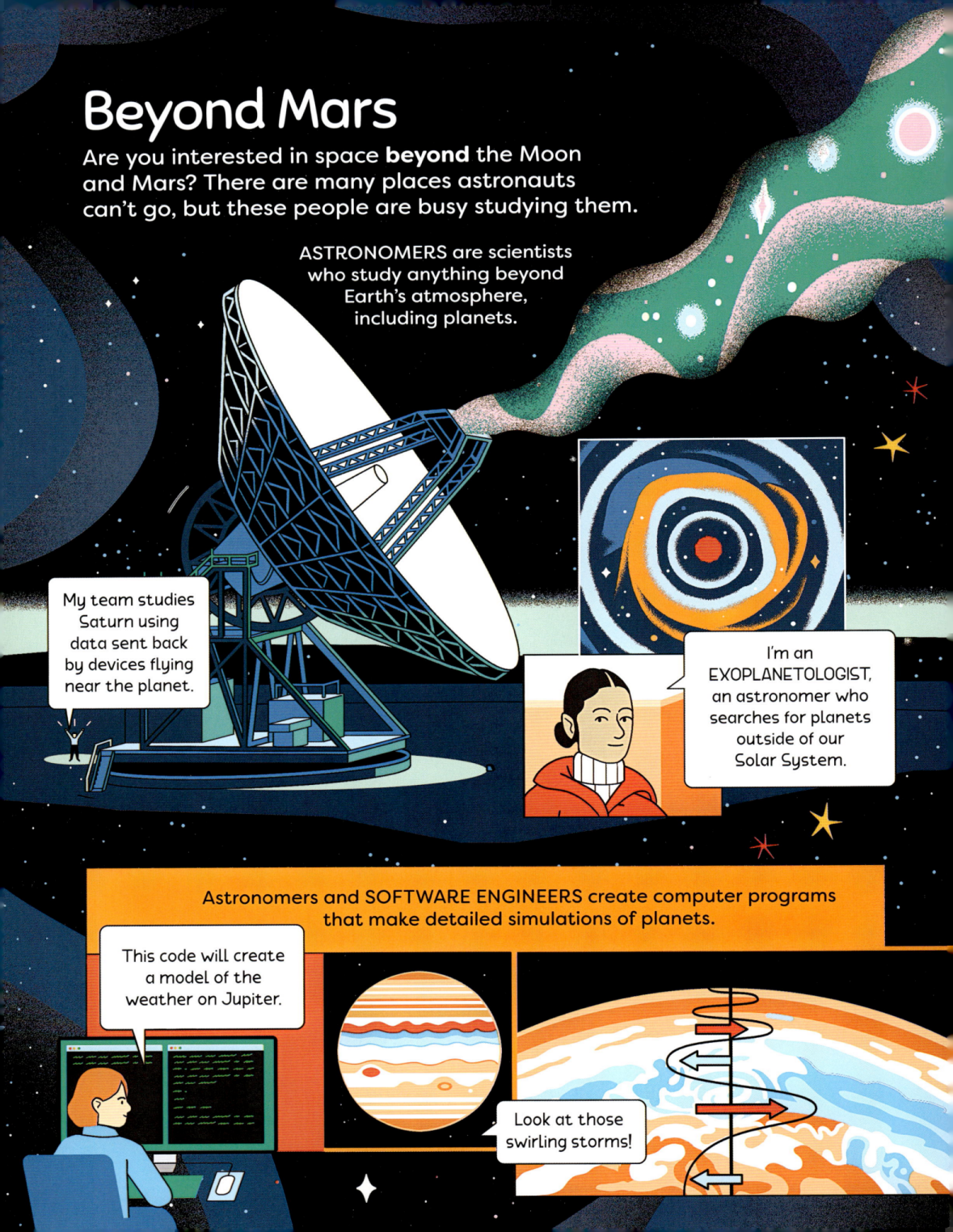

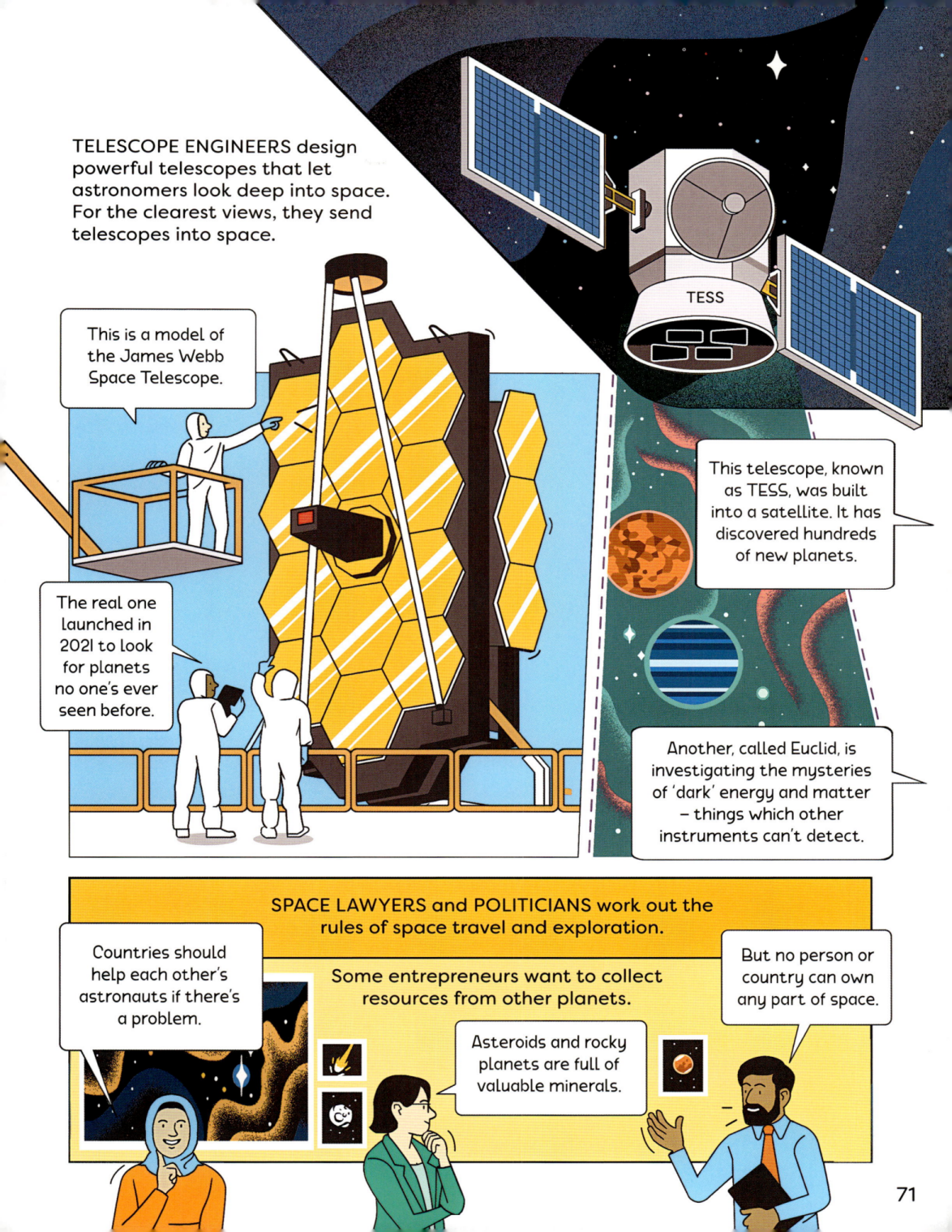

Space probes

To gain even more knowledge of space beyond our nearest planets, scientists and engineers send uncrewed devices called **probes**.

Once scientists and Mission Control have planned a mission, aerospace engineers start working on probe designs. This requires careful testing and planning.

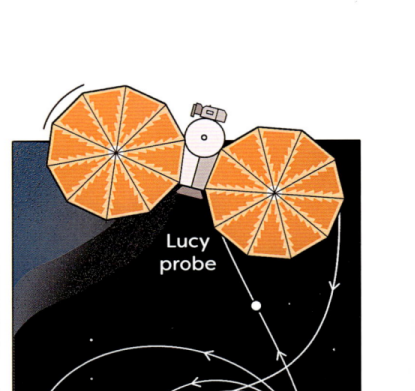

Lucy is a probe sent to study asteroids near Jupiter. The mission could take up to 12 years, so we had to calculate exactly how much fuel Lucy would need.

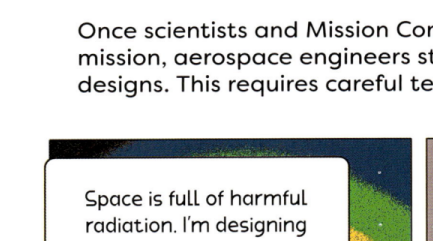

Space is full of harmful radiation. I'm designing probes made with a special material to shield them.

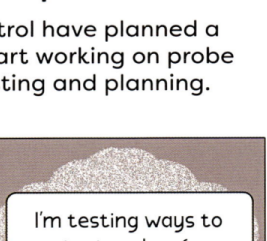

I'm testing ways to protect probes from destructive space dust and debris.

Other aerospace engineers build the rockets needed to launch probes.

This rocket is carrying a probe that will study the Sun.

After launch, teams of highly trained NAVIGATORS control probes from Earth.

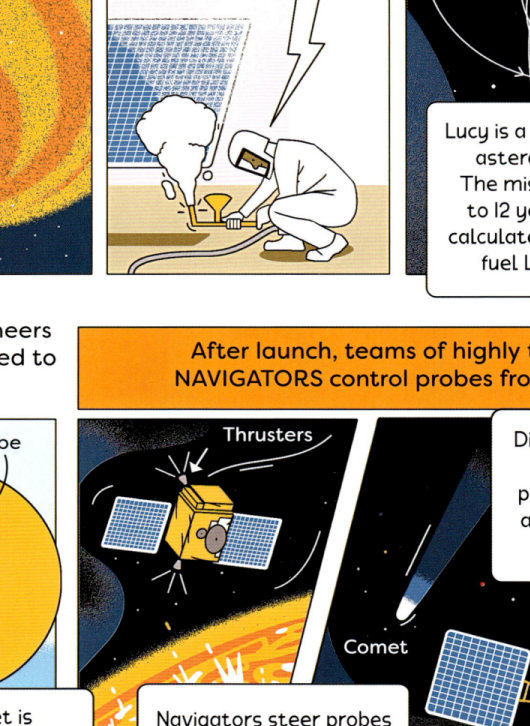

Navigators steer probes by remotely firing tiny engines called thrusters.

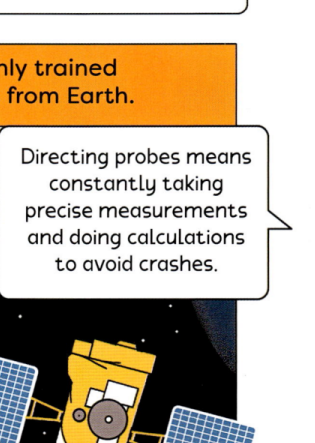

Directing probes means constantly taking precise measurements and doing calculations to avoid crashes.

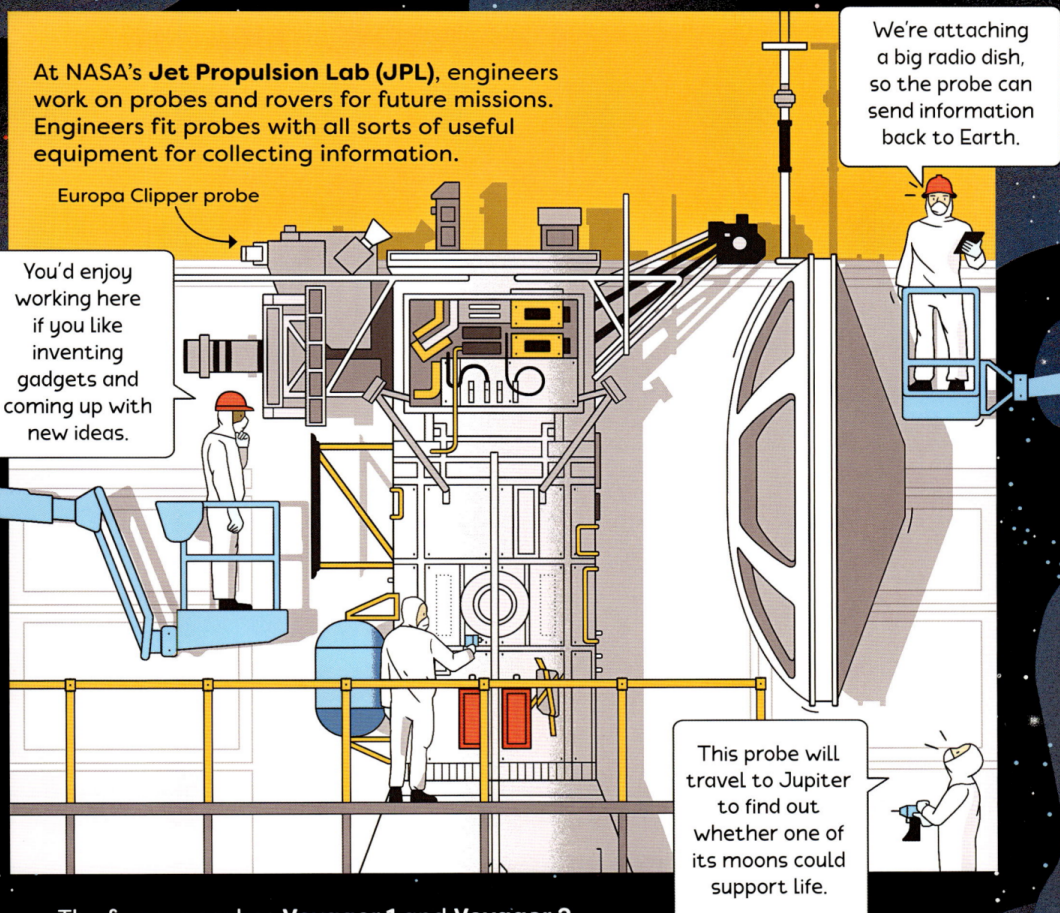

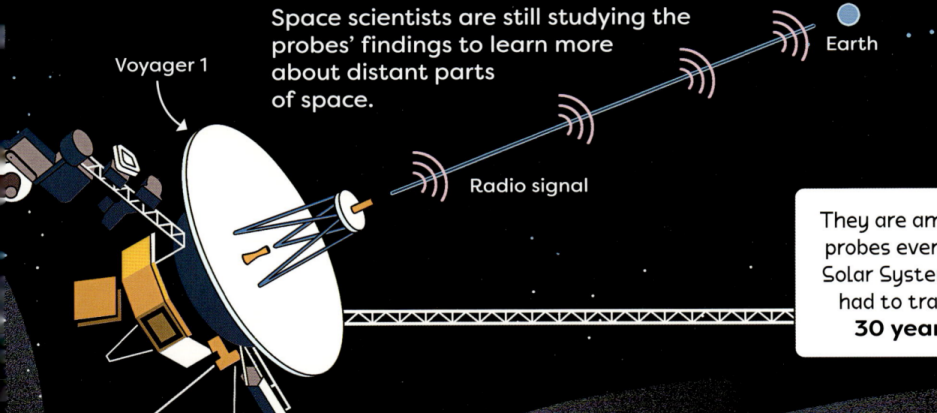

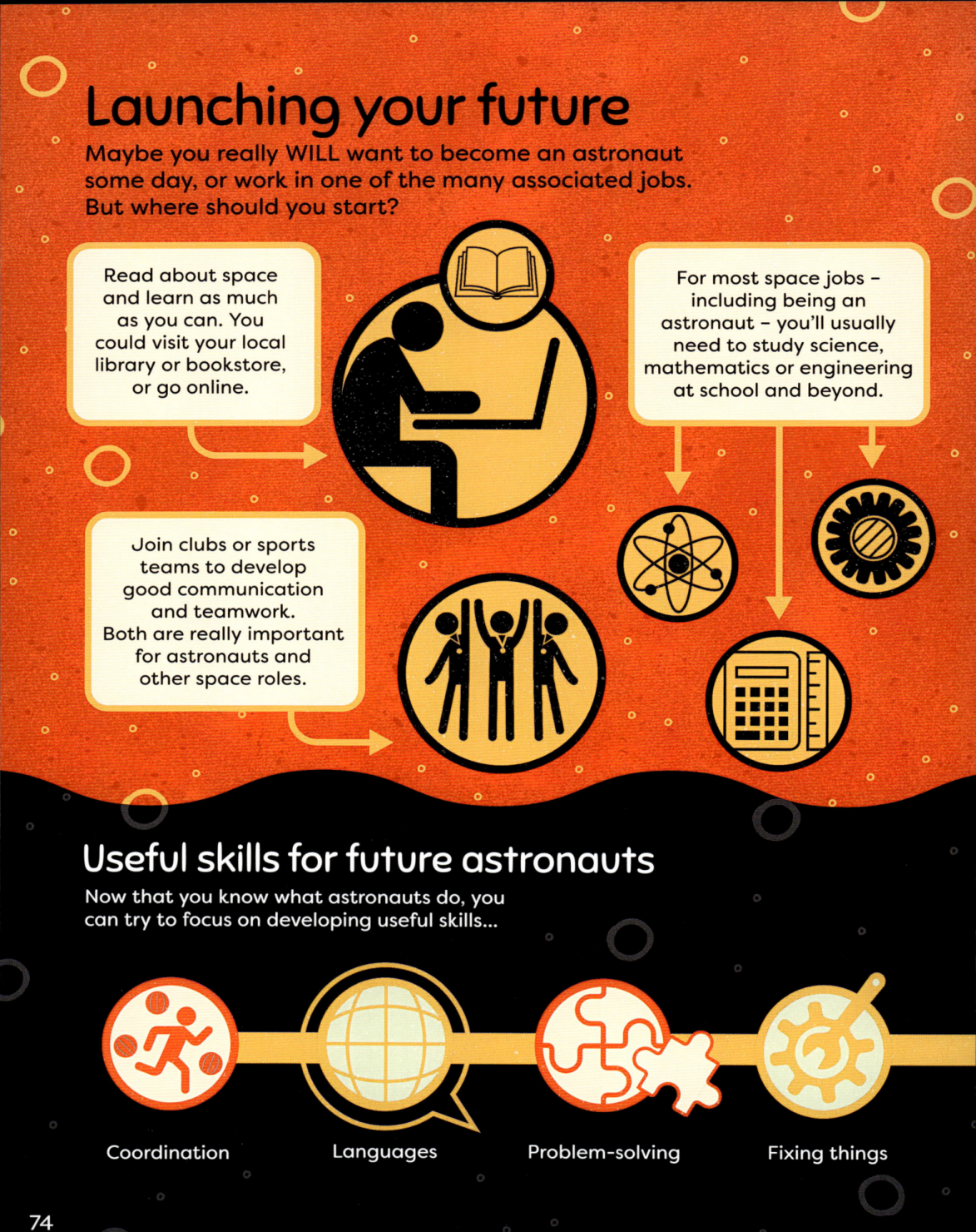

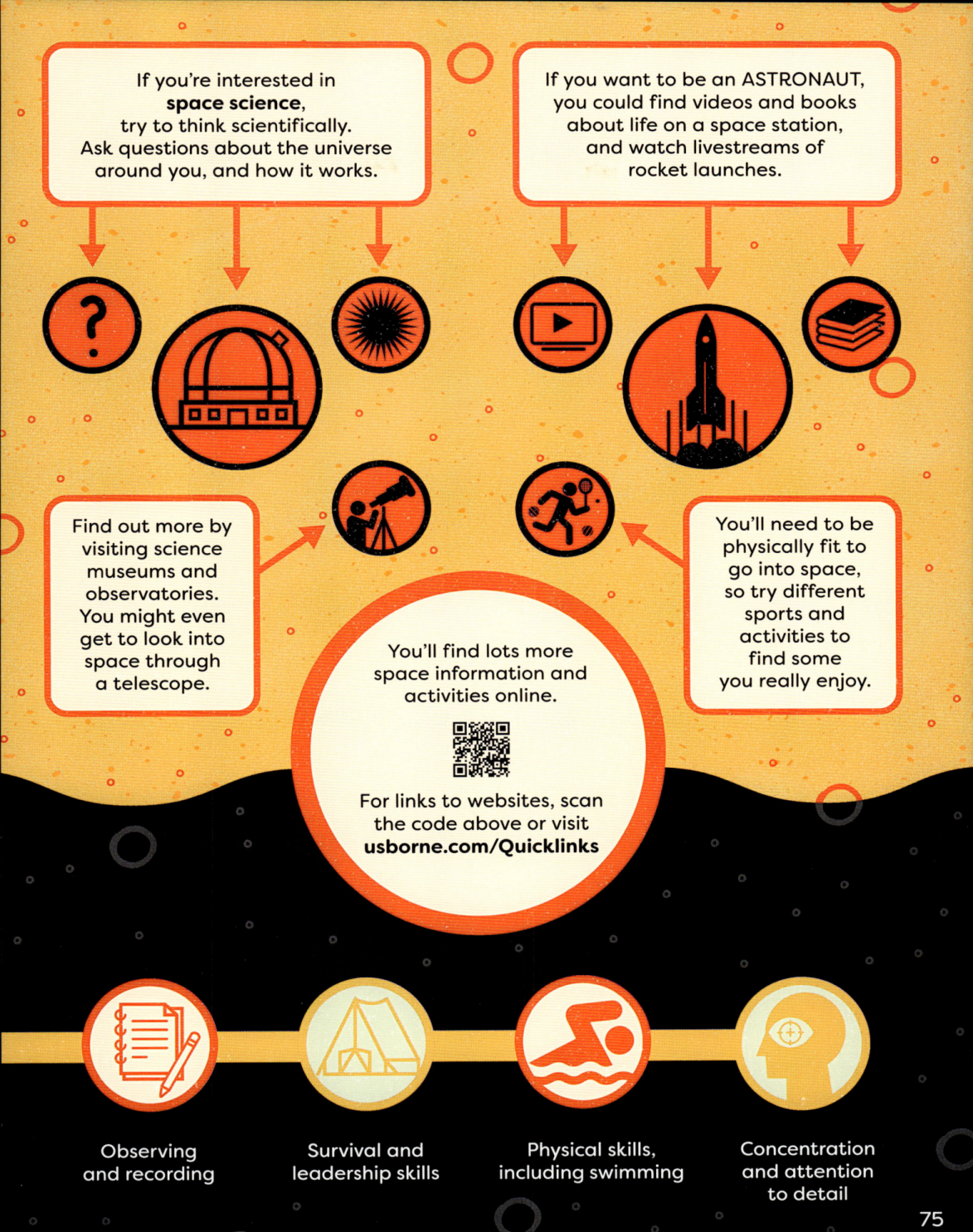

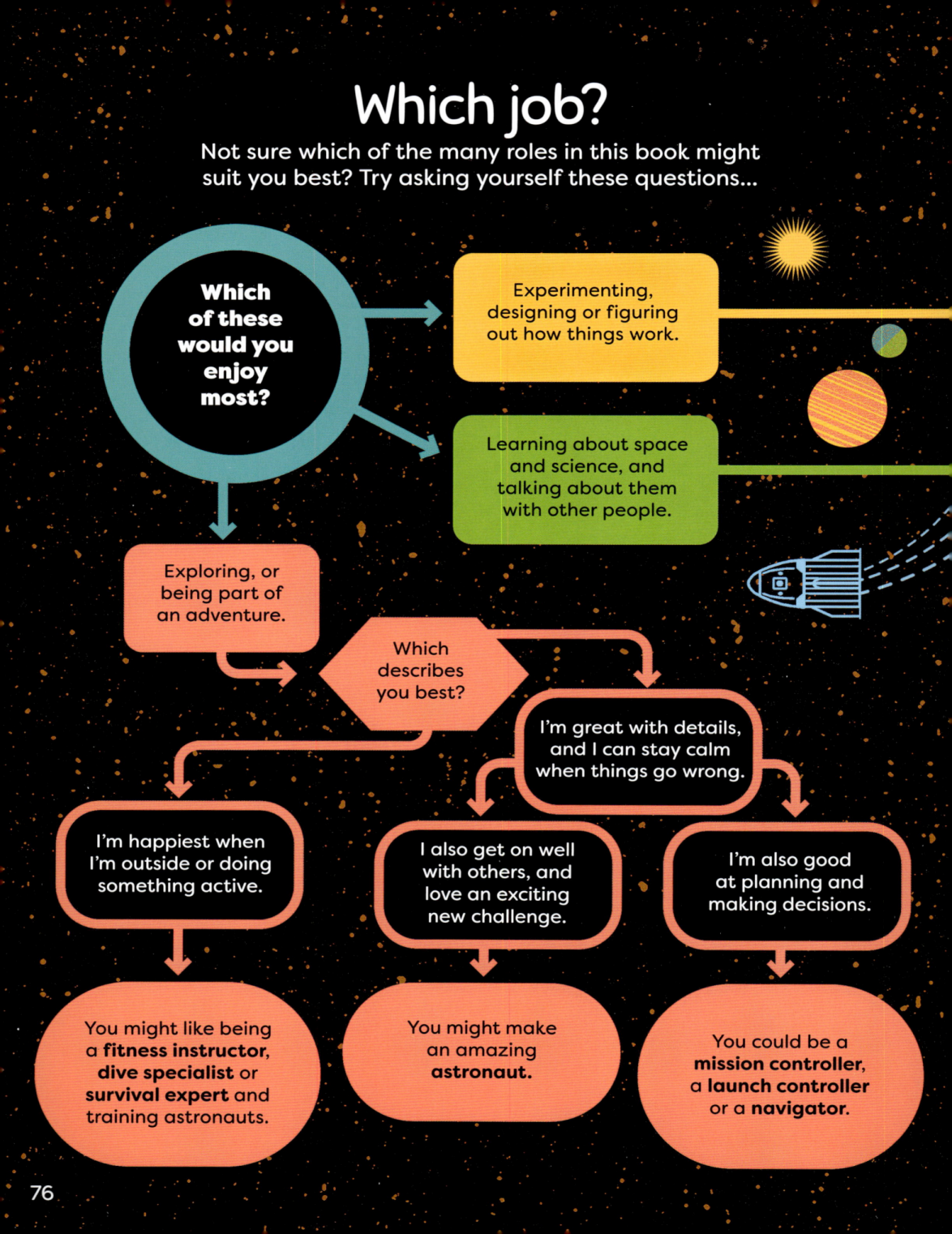

Jobs in the space industry

Here are all of the space jobs mentioned in this book. You can look them up in the index to find out which pages they're on.

AEROSPACE ENGINEERS design spacecraft and rockets.

ARTIFICIAL INTELLIGENCE (AI) ENGINEERS program rovers to think for themselves.

ASTROBIOLOGISTS study how space affects different creatures.

ASTROBOTANISTS work on growing plants in space.

ASTRODYNAMICS EXPERTS study how spacecraft are affected by different forces.

ASTRONAUTS travel into space.

ASTRONOMERS study stars, planets and everything else found in space.

AVIONICS EXPERTS design electrical systems for spacecraft.

BIOMEDICAL OFFICERS make sure astronauts stay healthy.

BIOMEDICAL SCIENTISTS study living human cells in space.

CAPSULE COMMUNICATORS (CAPCOM) communicate with astronauts during flights.

COMPUTER ENGINEERS and TECHNICIANS design and build computer systems for spacecraft.

DIVE SPECIALISTS help astronauts with underwater training.

DOCTORS carry out health checks on astronauts before and after missions.

EVA OFFICERS plan and control spacewalks.

EXOPLANETOLOGISTS search for planets outside our Solar System.

FAILURE ANALYSTS look at any problems with a spacecraft's structure.

FLIGHT CONTROLLERS oversee space flights and run space stations.

FLIGHT DIRECTORS are in charge of teams of flight controllers.

FLIGHT DYNAMICS OFFICERS plot and track spacecraft flight paths.

FOOD SCIENTISTS plan and pack the meals astronauts eat in space.

FUEL TECHNICIANS load rockets with fuel.

LAUNCH CONTROLLERS and TECHNICIANS oversee spacecraft launches.

LAUNCH DIRECTORS head up launch teams.

MATERIAL SCIENCE EXPERTS work out the best materials for building spacecraft.

MECHANICAL ENGINEERS design and build spacecraft and other space tech.

NAVIGATORS steer probes through space.

PROPULSION OFFICERS make sure a spacecraft's engines are working well.

PSYCHOLOGISTS study how living on another planet might affect people.

ROBOTICS ENGINEERS design robots for future space missions.

SOFTWARE ENGINEERS create computer programs for spacecraft and space science.

SPACE ARCHITECTS design space habitats.

SPACE LAWYERS work out the rules of space.

SPACE SUIT DESIGNERS design the suits astronauts wear in space.

SPECIALIST INSTRUCTORS teach trainee astronauts fitness, survival and language skills.

SUIT TECHNICIANS help astronauts put on their flight suits.

TELESCOPE ENGINEERS design telescopes to study space.

TEST CONTROLLERS oversee tests for new space equipment and trainees.

TEST ENGINEERS make sure spacecraft can handle the demands of space flight.

Index

advanced training, 14-15
aerospace engineers, 23, 24, 64, 72, 77, 78
Aquarius, 20-21
artificial intelligence (AI) engineers, 63, 67, 78
astrobiologists, 53, 56, 77, 78
astrobotanists, 53, 56, 77, 78
astrodynamics experts, 24, 78
astronomers, 63, 70-71, 77, 78
avionics experts, 24, 78

basic training, 10-11, 13, 61
biomedical experts, 43, 55, 77, 78

capsule communicator, 37, 78
China National Space Administration (CNSA), 7
communications, 21, 24, 58
computer engineers and technicians, 23, 24, 53, 58, 78
control room, 19
cosmonauts, 7, 49
crew vessel, 15, 24-25, 26, 28-29, 33-34, 38-39

dark matter, 71
Desert Research and Technology Studies (Desert RATS), 65
dive specialists, 9, 18-19, 76, 78, 79
doctors, 58, 60, 69, 77, 78

Earth scientists, 53, 57, 78
EVA officer, 41, 50-51, 78
European Space Agency (ESA), 6
exoplanetologists, 70, 77, 78
Extra Vehicular Mobility Unit (EMU), 15

failure analysts, 29, 77, 78
fire, 11, 12, 54
fitness, 9, 10, 45, 75
fitness instructors, 9, 10, 76, 78
flight controllers, 31, 36-37, 38-39, 41, 43, 51, 78
flight director, 36, 78
flight dynamics officer, 36, 39, 78
food, 12, 41-42, 48-49, 56, 69
food scientists, 41, 49, 77, 78
forces, 16, 23, 24
fuel technicians, 31, 34, 78

games, 33, 46, 55

health, 11, 41, 43, 45, 55, 60, 63, 69, 77
holoporting, 58

International Space Station (ISS), the, 6-7, 37, 39, 42, 51, 54-55, 56-57, 58

Japan Aerospace Exploration Agency (JAXA), 7
Jet Propulsion Lab (JPL), 73

Johnson Space Center, 69
Jupiter, 70, 72-73

language, 10
launch controllers, 31, 33, 76, 78
launch director, 35, 78
launch technicians, 31, 32, 78
lunar base camp, 64

Mars, 15, 66-67, 68-69
Mars Dune Alpha, 69
material science experts, 24, 78
mechanical engineers, 25, 26-27, 32, 77, 78
mechanics, 10, 39
meteorology, 10
microgravity, 16-17, 44-45, 46-47, 48, 54-55, 56
Mission Control, 36-37, 38-39, 43, 51, 60, 72
Moon, the, 6, 15, 59, 63, 64-65

National Aeronautics and Space Administration (NASA), 6, 14, 33, 44, 65, 67, 68-69, 73
naturalists, 53, 57, 78
navigation, 12, 24, 72
navigators, 63, 72, 76, 78
nuclear propulsion, 68

orbit, 7, 16, 39, 43, 68

parachutes, 11, 13, 60
photography, 11, 57, 67
physiology, 10
planes, 9, 11, 17, 26
plants, 54, 56, 64, 69
probes, 72-3, 77
propulsion officer, 37, 78
Project Artemis, 64
psychologists, 63, 69, 77, 78
public speaking, 11, 61

relaxation, 46
rescue teams, 12-13, 57
robotics engineers, 58, 66, 77, 78
robots, 58-9, 67
Astrobees, 58
Ingenuity, 67
Robonaut, 59
Valkyrie, 59
rockets, 10, 23, 24-25, 27, 28, 31, 32, 34-35, 36-37, 38, 68, 75, 77
fuel, 25, 31, 34, 38, 68-69, 72
launch, 10, 28, 32, 34-35, 38
Roscosmos, 7
rovers, 63, 65, 66-7, 73, 77
Perseverance, 67
Zhurong, 66

Saturn, 70
science experiments, 15, 54-55, 56-57, 58, 69, 77
shaker, the, 28
sea, 13, 20-21, 28, 60
sleep, 34, 47, 58, 65
software engineers, 70, 78
space architects, 63, 69, 77, 78
space lawyers, 71, 77, 78
space simulator, 29
space suit designers, 15, 50, 77, 78
space suits, 15, 50-51, 60
Space Vehicle Mock-Up Facility (SVMF), 14-15
spacecraft, 6, 10-11, 12-13, 14-15, 18-19, 24-25, 26-27, 28-29, 31, 32-33, 34-35, 36-37, 38-39, 42, 58, 60, 64, 66
assembly, 25-26
docking, 39, 42
flight testing, 28-29

spacewalks, 18, 41, 50-51, 69
suit technicians, 31, 33, 78
Sun, the, 24, 29, 72
super guppy, 26
survival experts, 12, 76
survival skills, 12-13, 75
swimming, 10, 13, 75

tardigrades, 56
telescopes, 71, 75
test engineers, 19, 23, 28-29, 77, 78
toilet, 14, 21, 44

washing, 47
water training, 9, 13, 18-19, 20-21
weather, 10, 33, 70

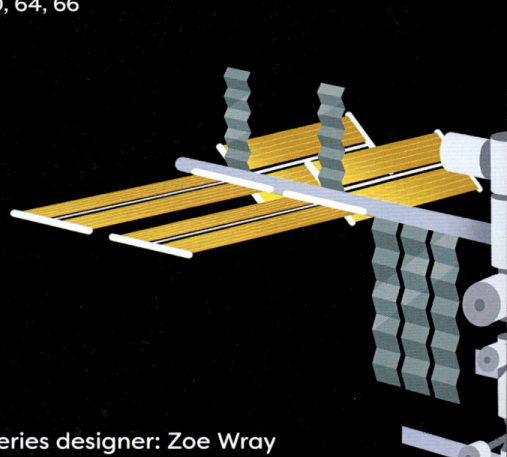

Series editor: Rosie Dickins Series designer: Zoe Wray

First published in 2024 by Usborne Publishing Limited, 83-85 Saffron Hill, London EC1N 8RT, United Kingdom. usborne.com Copyright © 2024 Usborne Publishing Limited. The name Usborne and the Balloon logo are registered trade marks of Usborne Publishing Limited. All rights reserved. No part of this publication may be reproduced, stored in a retrieval system or transmitted in any form or by any means without prior permission of the publisher. UE. Printed in UAE.

Usborne Publishing is not responsible and does not accept liability for the availability or content of any website other than its own, or for any exposure to harmful, offensive or inaccurate material which may appear on the Web. Usborne Publishing will have no liability for any damage or loss caused by viruses that may be downloaded as a result of browsing the sites it recommends.